I0541190

E.M. KEELAN

SAGE'S ✝ CROSS
BOOK ONE
CROWN OF THORNS

Red Quill PRESS

Cover design, interior book design,
eBook design, and editing
by Blue Harvest Creative
www.blueharvestcreative.com

CROWN OF THORNS

Copyright © 2015 E.M. Keelan

All rights reserved. Except as permitted under the U.S. Copyright Act of 1976, no part of this publication may be reproduced, distributed, or transmitted in any form or by any means, or stored in a database or retrieval system, without prior written permission of the publisher.

This book is a work of fiction. The characters, incidents, and dialogue are drawn from the author's imagination and are not to be construed as real. Any resemblance to actual events or persons, living or dead, is entirely coincidental.

Published by
Red Quill Press

ISBN-13: 978-0692383995
ISBN-10: 0692383999

Visit the author at:
Website: *www.emkeelan.com & www.bhcauthors.com*
Facebook: *www.facebook.com/emkeelan*
Twitter: *www.twitter.com/emkeelan*

Visit the author's Facebook page
by scanning the QR code.

This book is dedicated to my wife and daughter,
as well as those who inspired me, thank you for being my muses.

CROWN OF THORNS

ONE

JT Steele stood in front of the small crowd that had been invited to his pay-per-view event. They were out in a forest in the middle of nowhere. Behind him was a large cave with two old stone doors covered in a language that no one understood. There were two heavy chains leading from the doors that were attached to heavy-duty construction trucks.

"Ladies and gentlemen..." JT said, smiling. This secret was going to change the world. "You have seen the research. This is a true gateway to Hell. And tonight, we are going to open the gates."

Hazel looked toward Rowan and Sage. "Doesn't he know things don't work out well when you talk like that?"

Sage kept her eyes on the set and all the moving pieces. The scaffolding looked precarious, and the lights beamed down on JT, making him look almost effervescent. She saw a few members of the production crew look at each other as though wondering what they'd gotten themselves into. She watched all the executives in their suits as they talked about how much money they were going to make off this adventure. She and her friends had been invited as special guests of Mr. Steele. The crowd hung on his every word. She wrapped her arms around herself, warding off the chill in the air.

"He doesn't care," Rowan said. She knew a thing or two about JT. She knew there were two types of investigators: ones that go for the truth and try to help people and others that are in it for the thrill. JT Steele was the second type. "All he is concerned with is how much he'll get paid if they do find something. So why are we here? If whatever is on the other side mauls him, that's one last bad influence we have to worry about."

Sage had met JT on several occasions at supernatural conventions, and she'd never really cared for him. This, however, was the first time she'd actually gotten to see him work. They had talked in the past; he'd told her he thought there was something off about her group of friends. "We are here to observe," she told Rowan. "If anything supernatural does come out of that gate, I want to be the first to see it."

"Then can we fight it?" Rowan asked.

"No, we are here to watch and make sure this whole thing isn't one big scam. I know plenty of people who are expecting it to be. Besides, we can't blow our cover with millions of people watching."

Their work was best done in the shadows. If anyone knew what hid in the dark, there would be chaos.

"Makes sense to me," said Hazel. "I wasn't in the mood to fight anyway."

Rowan glared at her. "When are you ever in the mood to fight?"

"Really? Coming from the person who is supposed to be training me? Sorry I'm not all warrior like you."

JT began pacing up and down the set. It was hard to tell if he was nervous or simply working the crowd. He made his way in between the two trucks and motioned for them to start their engines. It was time for the big reveal. Sage noticed two of the cameramen glancing at each other. It was clear that even those working on the set didn't know what to expect. JT was the only one with any confidence about what was behind those doors. He turned to the two trucks and shouted, "It's time. Open the gate." Sage saw fear flash across his eyes for just a moment. That was when she began to worry.

The motors roared as they struggled to go forward. The producers and executives froze, watching mesmerized along with everyone else.

There were a couple of people who were filming on their cell phones, and Sage knew there would be leaked footage if anything happened and this show never aired. A loud cry sent a chill down Sage's spine as the doors began to open.

The smell of sulfur wafted over the crowd of people. Rowan gagged. She knew this smell too well. "We need to leave."

"What's going on?" Hazel asked. It wasn't like Rowan to suggest retreat.

"I can't stand it. Don't you smell that?" Rowan covered her mouth with her arm.

Sage saw panic begin to wrap its icy fingers around Rowan, her eyes wide and pleading. "Let's go." The three of them turned and started to navigate through the crowd toward their truck, trying to figure out the best plan for the situation. Especially since they didn't know what was going on.

"There's something coming out of the gates," a cameraman yelled.

Sage stopped, but something in her gut kept her from turning around. From the corner of her eye, she could see five figures come out of the open doors. They were moving fast. A few people from the crowd started backing toward the exits. Others couldn't seem to take their eyes off the gate and the five shapes emerging from it.

"All of our weapons are in the truck," Sage said. "We need to head that way. This has the potential to get ugly fast, and we may have to protect the innocent."

The beings were now fully out of the gate. They were statuesque, strong, and terribly beautiful.

"Freedom," the first male being said, and Sage froze. She recognized the voice and immediately she was hit by waves of emotion ranging everywhere from rage to fear. She suddenly realized there was a chance that her quest for revenge was going to have an ending.

The beings moved toward JT, and in the blink of an eye, he was on the ground bleeding from a fist-sized hole in his stomach. The crowd scattered at the sight of JT's fallen body, screams filling the air.

"What's going on?" said Hazel, turning toward Sage who was still frozen. "Sage, we have to go. Now."

Rowan grabbed Sage's arm, and Sage finally came back to. The screams increased as the creatures caught up with those too slow to escape. Equipment was getting turned over and lights broke in explosions of glass. After a few moments of shoving through the crowd and getting through busted-up equipment, Rowan, Hazel, and Sage finally reached their truck. When they had a second to catch their breath, Rowan looked at Sage and asked, "What was going on with you back there?"

Before Sage could answer, a streak of light crossed the sky and slammed the doors to the gate closed.

Rowan looked to Sage. "Michael?" she asked.

Sage nodded. "Without a doubt. He's the only one that would be sent to get some control of this thing before it got too out of hand."

"What do you mean 'too out of hand?'" Hazel then realized who they were talking about. "Did you just say the Archangel Michael showed up and closed the gate?"

"Yes," Sage said matter-of-factly. "It was him. I've seen him help out in situations but never as close as this. It meant they knew how bad the situation could have got. We're lucky only five escaped. Best thing for us to do right now is to get out of here, regroup, and figure out what happened."

"Why were you so spooked when that fallen angel spoke?" Hazel questioned.

"You mean the one that took out JT?"

"Yeah?"

"That was my father."

THOMAS WAS A new breed of vampire that was slowly getting noticed by others of their kind. He was a breed that had forward thinking. He knew the human race was obsessed with them, so why not use that to his advantage? The only problem was the old vampires who were sitting on top of the food chain. "It's worked for hundreds of years and it will continue to work now" was their reply to every suggestion of change.

Thomas watched as those vampires discussed plans for the Summit of the Vampire Clans. He hated every one of them and their way of thinking. Hiding in the shadows was no way for someone with their abilities to live. He looked at the one who had created him, and he saw a barbarian who had taken advantage of him, seducing him with the vampire lore.

Every promise Soanso made had yet to come to fruition. Thomas was better than broken promises. He could be so much more than just his creator's minion.

Thomas looked at his watch. He was running late for his job, which was another thing the elders didn't understand. The new breed of vampires believed they needed to make their money as well as maintain some sort of normalcy. They believed they were more civilized than the elders who came before them. They never attacked the innocent or hunted for their prey in the shadows.

Thomas caught Soanso's eye. His creator nodded, and Thomas left their lair. The meeting hall was inside a large warehouse that doubled as a nightclub. It was a short walk to work, but he enjoyed any moment by himself he could get. It was moments like this that Thomas was able to take in all the sights and smells of the city. For those few blocks, he felt alive again.

The elders had their issues with the youth movement, especially since it was gaining strength. Without a leader, though, the newer breed was vulnerable to attack. Thomas knew this was a topic that the elders planned on discussing at the Summit.

He thought about his options as he walked into the Blood Bar where he worked. It was a simple, unobtrusive bar; most people didn't even notice it as they passed by on the street. It was where everyone in the youth movement hung out. He walked into the club and went through his normal walk-through. He always got there early enough to see who was around before he started working. He went over to the balcony and surveyed the area. Then he saw her.

She was unlike anyone he'd ever seen before. There was a radiance about her, and he knew right away that she wasn't human. He wasn't sure if she was a vampire. Something made her different from everyone else around her. He wondered why she would set herself up like that, standing in the crowd of people, unmoving. It was risking discovery. She'd be destroyed quickly. He went back downstairs, and they made eye contact. She smiled at him. Her gaze was intoxicating. She motioned for him to sit down and took a seat next to him.

"It looks like we have some things to talk about," she said. "We could make each other so happy."

"Really?" Thomas was surprised by how forward she was.

"By the way," she said, extending her hand, "my name is Meditrina."

AS SAGE DROVE off the set, Hazel asked from the backseat, "How is that thing your father?"

Sage made a hard turn out to the makeshift parking lot. "I'm not human."

"Right." Suddenly Hazel shot forward in her seat like an arrow. "What did you just say?" she asked in disbelief.

"It's true," said Rowan. "She is a Nephilim."

Sage was distracted, trying to find the quickest way off the set, not having much luck so far. "I'm half angel, half human," she explained. A figure appeared in front of the truck, moving quickly in their direction. Sage stepped on the gas when she saw it.

"Sage, what are you doing?" Hazel grabbed Sage's shoulder.

"I'm just going to say hello to my father."

"By running him down?" Hazel asked. She checked the buckle on her seat belt and pulled it tight.

Rowan grinned and braced for impact. "Sage has some daddy issues."

Sage pushed harder on the gas. When they were close enough, Sage and her father made eye contact. He smiled at her and then disappeared. Sage lost control of the truck and slammed into a parked car. Shaken by the impact, the girls in the back tried to collect themselves while Sage got out, inspecting the damage.

After managing to pull themselves together, Rowan and Hazel got out of the truck. Rowan said, "The good thing is no one got seriously hurt."

"Why would you try to run your father down like that?" Hazel asked.

"He killed my mother." Sage slammed her hands down on the hood of the damaged truck.

TWO

The candles of the room flickered as Meditrina pushed opened the oak doors. "Were you planning on starting this gathering without me?"

The vampires turned toward her, shocked at this intrusion into their secret meeting hall. She glided toward them with the determined grace of an ice dancer, her crimson train fanning out behind her.

Thomas glanced at the empty chair of his master and did his best to hide the grin that was spreading across his face. He looked over at Meditrina and tried to follow the other's lead as she entered the private summit. There was a plan in play, and he knew he had to keep his cool. The only problem was that this plan came from someone who enjoyed the terror she caused. He hated the elders and their old ways, but he was afraid of Meditrina and the lengths to which she would go.

Thomas watched as she sat down in his master's empty chair and took in her surroundings. She looked far younger than any of the others at the table, but her porcelain skin and black eyes betrayed ancient powers.

She took in the old clan heads and laughed as if she were keeping the punch line of a joke to herself. "If you are wondering whether Jacob is going to show up, I wouldn't hold your breath. Let's just say that he is indisposed. In fact," she said, "didn't he typically wear this?" She held up

Jacob's ancient amulet showing his clan leadership. Her laughter took on an edge of madness. "Isn't the person who wears this a clan leader?" She gracefully draped it around her neck then poured herself a drink. "Well, consider this his resignation."

An arrogance that could only come from living several lifetimes emanated out of Elder Christian Oleander. He was the oldest of the clan leaders, and the most powerful. His charcoal black hair hung down to his shoulders, bits of gray showing here and there.

"Just who in the hell are you?"

Thomas jumped as Christian slammed his goblet of wine down on the table. He didn't know if it was from surprise or that his adrenaline was kicking in from all the excitement.

Fury burned in Christian's eyes. "Your explanation had better be good, because my curiosity is the only thing keeping me from snapping your neck like a twig."

A chill of fear shot through Thomas's spine and down to his toes. He'd always known this was risky, but he hadn't realized until now how high that risk was. He tried to push the fear back out of his body, focusing instead on the task at hand. Meditrina's plan, the plan that he had helped put into motion, would be considered treason to his clan. But when all was finished it would be the birth of a new order. He was going to be at the top of the food chain. That was something he could get used to.

Meditrina stood up, her mahogany hair falling luxuriously over her bare shoulders. She looked around the room. "Gentlemen, my name is Meditrina." She paused, enjoying the varied reactions in the room.

"The Roman goddess of wine and health," said Jack Beaumont. He had lived several lifetimes, although he wasn't quite as old as Christian. "An interesting choice. The question is: how well do you live up to the namesake?"

Meditrina smiled, searching the crowd for the speaker. "I see you know me, then. I am impressed. I like a man who knows his history. It's a way to make sure the same mistakes aren't repeated. Because of that, I think I'll kill you last." She turned back to the rest of the room. "As I was saying, my name is Meditrina. I am the new head of the Seventh Clan." Someone laughed, and a murmur spread across the table.

"How could this young vampire have destroyed Jacob? He is three hundred and twenty-seven years old." Thomas recognized him right away. It was Samuel Fey, a vampire that had known Jacob for most of his life.

"Correction," said Meditrina, "he *was* three hundred and twenty-seven. The only thing he is right now is dust." She laughed and casually took a sip from the glass in front of her.

"This is murder." One of the clan leaders stood up. "There is no reason we should even allow her to sit at this table with us. This is not how things are done within the clans."

Samuel spoke up. "This is an outrage. We have ways and rules. This is not how it's done."

"Clan leaders fall when they have someone angry enough at them. We have all made enemies in our time," Leopold added.

"To top it off, she is a woman," Emmanuel Lefevre said. "A woman hasn't set foot in this room for hundreds of years."

Many agreed, and sides quickly formed as they debated and argued.

"My friends, we all need to sit down and discuss this like civilized people," Christian said. Although he tried to gain control, any semblance of order had unraveled.

This was the first time they had disagreed in years. Meditrina worked quickly. She used their weaknesses and planned to use their vanity and hunger for power to her advantage. With Thomas's help, she had known everything in advance to make the leaders vulnerable. In the end, Thomas knew that this was only a taste of Meditrina's power. He was glad she came to him in the bar that night, wanting to make his dream a reality.

Meditrina circled the table, subtly touching each chair as she walked by. As she drew nearer to Thomas, he saw her slip a device—no bigger than a credit card—onto the back of each chair.

"Gentlemen," she said, causing a hush to fall over the room. "I am here to discuss the future of the vampire race. The way we live is so boring and is not even close to the potential we have. We deserve better. I am here to talk to you about vampires taking their rightful place."

Thomas knew that the old world was about to change, and that he alone had been granted access to the new one. With the new order Meditrina would put in place, he wouldn't be held back again.

"Our rightful place as what?" asked Samuel.

"As supreme rulers of this world," she said. She looked at each of the clan heads individually. "Aren't vampires the equivalent of the Devil's angels? Isn't this the place where the Devil is supposed to be in control?" Meditrina paused, letting her comment sink in. A few members began nodding but remained silent. Thomas could tell many agreed with Meditrina but weren't interested in stepping out of their comfort zones. They began to whisper amongst themselves as Meditrina glided around the table, looking at each of the clan heads as she passed them. "Well, isn't he?"

Thomas pushed his chair back and stood up. "Yes, he is," he said. Her trap was set. He was simply playing his part. He knew no one wanted to be the first to agree with Meditrina. It was his job to fan the flames and turn it into a fire of disagreement. He was hoping there were others that saw things the same way. "Surely by now the elders realize there is a youth movement among the clans. We see the potential we have and are tired of living in the shadows. We've waited long enough for a chance to step up. We need someone to lead us to the place where we belong. We are the Devil's angels, and it is time we started acting it." The clan leaders all stared at him as he spoke out of turn. Thomas looked back at each one of them. He knew if this failed he would die.

"Good, clever boy. Here's someone who sees the bigger picture. Why shouldn't we take our rightful places? Shouldn't we serve a master that is going to be good to us and treat us like the powerful beings that we are?"

"Those angels left heaven. They challenged God and look where it got them." A hunched-over man named Julius with liver spots on his hands spoke up. Meditrina's gaze seemed to bore right through him, and for a moment her beauty faded.

"That's because they didn't have the right people leading them," she said. "Lucifer had the right idea, but he didn't have the right beings in the position to make it happen."

"So you are expecting us to do better than they did," another voice shouted. Laughter rippled through the room. Meditrina joined in.

"No, of course not. Why would I expect a silly thing like that?" The mischievous grin returned to her face. Her previous beauty was deteriorating, leaving behind only evil. Thomas saw the change, and the elders squirmed in their chairs as they saw the same thing.

"My dear, unless you can get to the point of your little speech, you need to take a seat," Christian said, trying to take back control. "Even though it is against the way we do things around here, since you have the amulet, we will accept—for now—the fact that you are the new leader of the Seventh Clan. But that will come at a price; you will have to face the court and explain your case." He looked over to Thomas with disappointment. "The same goes for you. We have all treated you as family and to disrespect us like this is uncalled for."

Thomas looked down at the ground, hiding his grin. "I understand."

"Whatever you need to do," Meditrina said chillingly.

"What we cannot accept, however, is your crazy idea about becoming the supreme race. We have some other things to discuss, so make your decision." Even though Meditrina was controlling the conversation, this was still their show.

Meditrina continued to walk around the room. With the dexterity of a street magician, a remote appeared in her hands. "Gentlemen, I have already made my decision." She hit the button on the remote and a bolt of electricity shot through each chair. The vampires convulsed and attempted to escape. Meditrina laughed. "First of all, I would suggest using wooden chairs at your next meeting. Although the metal ones do make my little toy work so much better. It's also pretty handy for keeping you in your place, in case you hadn't noticed. Now, to answer a question you asked earlier. You wondered who I thought I was, walking into this great meeting, demanding respect. I am the new leader of the unified clans. Yes, I did say unified. You are right: I am not like you. I am a fallen angel who just happens to be a vampire. So the comment made earlier about Lucifer failing because he didn't have the right beings helping him? I know firsthand. I was there.

"Now, gentlemen," she said, prowling around the table like a lioness stalking a gazelle, "you need to understand something. I have no intention of letting you have any of the power that I talked about." Meditrina continued to toy with the clan leaders, sending the occasional shock to remind them that she was in control. "I'm going to take it all for myself, since it seems like none of you are interested in having it. My plan is simple. I will destroy all of you in one night and take full control." Meditrina looked around, power radiating from her body like a blinding light.

She spoke in the direction of the opened double doors and noticed that several others had gathered. She smiled at them. "My children, I am feeling a little lonely out here. Why don't you come and join me?" Two-dozen young vampires walked into the room. They took their positions throughout the room. The vampires that sat trapped at the table watched, horrified, as the odds slowly moved out of their favor.

"This is the beginning of a new movement for the entire vampire race. The old way of thinking is done. This is the dawn of a new day," said Meditrina, gesturing to the new arrivals. Once all the younger vampires were in position, two more walked in: a woman and a man wearing red and gold ceremonial robes. They walked toward Meditrina to present her with a golden chalice covered with jewels that glinted in the candlelight. They also gave her a matching curved dagger. When the dagger was revealed, the vampires still stuck in their chairs became visibly agitated. One of them managed to break free and ran for the doors. The young vampires swarmed around him like vultures on carrion.

Thomas knew it was the last time he would see him. He knew the other elders would go the same way. The clan leaders who had become family to him were going to perish and there wasn't a thing that he could do about it.

"Excellent, my friends," Meditrina said. "We now have our first sacrifice for the greater good." Within a few seconds, the horde had stripped the clothes off him and lifted him above their heads. The clan heads doubled their efforts to escape.

At the sight of the sacrifice, Meditrina seemed to transform. The angel in her was gone; she was pure vampire now. She kept smiling. Thomas recognized the look: she was hungry. Meditrina raised the dagger and chalice and began to speak in tongues no human was meant to understand. The twelve-member horde lowered the sacrifice.

Meditrina began to address everyone in the room. "My name is Meditrina," she said. "In this world where good and evil battle, I have become the embodiment of each. I am a warrior of both sides. I am an angel. I am what was once good. I am now a vampire, taking on the qualities of what is evil. In the end, aren't the two one and the same?"

Members of the twelve nodded in agreement.

"Tonight is the first step toward higher enlightenment. Tonight we claim our place as the superior species by unifying ourselves under one ruler."

The horde cheered, and she motioned them to raise the body of the vampire they had captured.

"I am known as Meditrina, the goddess of wine. The wine of this goddess is blood, and tonight the blood of these former leaders will be flowing." In one swift, powerful motion, Meditrina took the jeweled dagger and ran it across the vampire's throat. His blood arced back at her, but she didn't flinch. It splattered her skin like drizzle before a storm.

The vampire horde cheered and begged to share in the blood.

Meditrina smiled and lifted the golden chalice into the crimson stream. She held the chalice high then took a long drink from it. The blood spilled down her neck as she drank, and the horde inched closer to her.

"Easy, my children," she said. "We have plenty more. We still have five vampires that need to be drained of their blood. There will be enough to share when I am done with them."

Thomas felt sick to his stomach. He understood the need to feed and had felt it himself in the past, but this was just gruesome. His stomach turned as he watched the slaughter. Each of the five remaining vampires were drained of their blood, leaving just enough that they could still watch the festivities. Then she drank from them one by one, gaining their knowledge and power. The tangy iron scent, mixed with sweat and fear, made Thomas gag. Meditrina inhaled deeply, her body shaking and tingling with anticipation.

The horde feasted on whatever was tossed their way, and Meditrina continued to drink. Soon the carpet was soaked and Meditrina's minions ran across it like children running through puddles in a rainstorm. She made her way back to the top of the table with the chalice. The vampire horde looked up at her. The beauty that was once Meditrina was gone; the vampire in her was completely in control. Her dress was plastered to her body, almost indistinguishable from her skin. She was now their queen.

Thomas hadn't seen a bloodbath like this coming. He had wanted Meditrina to eliminate the old rule and bring in a new one. He knew that she was more powerful than any of the elders. He thought she would do it clean and simple. All he wanted was the new way of thinking to have a say. Never had he imagined it ending in a slaughterhouse, or her taking control of all the clans. Except it was too late. He was the one that gave her the "in" that she had needed.

He caught his breath and slowly made his way outside. It was his turn once again. He knew what was next, although he didn't understand the reasoning behind it. He needed to deliver on his end of the plan. Otherwise he was afraid he'd end up like the now-dead clan leaders. He had to deliver Sage McKenzie and her team to Meditrina.

THREE

Hazel sat on the back bumper of a black, high-end Chevy Avalanche and punched things into her tablet. She pushed her glasses up her nose and looked at Rowan, who was gathering some gear. Only ten days had passed since she'd joined the team, and she was still feeling out her partners. She was realizing how little she knew about Rowan. Sage had left the two of them to finish cleaning up what was left from the last mission. Rowan must have felt Hazel looking at her, because she looked up and met her eyes. Hazel quickly looked back down at her tablet. She thought about waving awkwardly, but was saved by her phone ringing. She put the phone on speaker. "Sage, when are you going to join the modern world and get yourself an iPhone like everyone else?"

"That's the problem," Sage said. "Everyone else has one of them so security is going to be an issue." Sage still used burner phones for security purposes.

"Not if I jailbreak it." Hazel knew she was a good hacker and didn't have a problem backing it up. "You let me jailbreak it then I can put what you need on it."

Rowan cast a disparaging look Hazel's way. Hazel caught the look and shrugged. "But we can talk about that later. Why are you checking in?"

"Just wanted to see how close you guys were to wrapping up," Sage said.

Hazel answered, "We're tying up a few loose ends but it looks like everything is back to normal and any trace of us coming into this city will be as good as gone."

"Good. Wrap everything up and get back on the road so you can meet up with me. I need to go check on some messages I've been getting from a vampire I know."

"But aren't they—"

"Thomas is a spoiled, perverted dog." Sage's admission to her true feelings about Thomas caught Hazel totally off guard. Rowan shook her head and walked off. "He keeps offering me the world if I let him turn me, but I've told him time and time again: undead is not my thing." She paused for a second and took a deep breath before continuing. "Still, I need to check this out. If this is real, then there could be some problems."

"Wow," Hazel said. "I was just going to say 'aren't they evil.'"

"I'll send you the final coordinates when I get there," Sage said and hung up. Hazel sat in stunned silence for a moment, trying to figure out what had just happened.

Rowan came back around the truck and looked at Hazel. "When she gets all girly like that, she's your problem."

"Why do you say that?" Hazel said, smirking.

"I don't do girly or emotions. I fight. That's it."

"Oh, so you're the big bad warrior then." Hazel enjoyed the opportunity to tease Rowan a little.

"Hell, you're lucky I'm actually talking to you. Get in the truck before I decide to drive off with you hanging on the back."

FOR SAGE, THE open road was a place to really put her foot down; it was a place to clear her head after a mission. Battling fallen angels took a lot out of her. Sage cut and weaved through the traffic on her custom chopper. She made her way to the next rest stop and pulled in. She slid off the bike, undid her earth-toned riding jacket, and scanned the area. There was a family sitting at a nearby picnic table eating lunch. A little girl who looked to be about seven eyed Sage up. Sage cast her a smile, thinking how oblivious she was to the things that went bump in the night. Hazel's face came to mind at that thought; she was fresh to the world and to the evil that they were fighting. Sage's mind wandered to the conversation she'd had with Hazel when she'd brought her on the team.

It hadn't been the first time she'd had to find someone to fill a position. It usually ended with them leaving after Sage had fulfilled her end. She was looking for loyalty, and she'd had to come up with a very specific way to test people. She asked the potential teammates some questions, and it all came down to the offer in the end. Only one person had ever passed the test: Rowan. The recent generations of youth could handle the battles but weren't interested in loyalty. One person in the decades that Sage had been doing this was not enough.

This was a first for Sage: filling the role of someone who had died in battle. Their old teammate, Victoria, had been a good friend and a trusted ally. She was going to be hard to replace, but war meant casualties. It was time to move on.

"Why me?" Hazel had asked, her blue eyes wide.

"I understand what you went through and the sacrifices you had to make, especially for your sister," Sage said. "The fact that Dr. McPeek took your gift and turned it into a weapon was wrong and unfair to you. You have carried that cross long enough. Let me carry it for you. Let me teach you how to use what you have the right way."

How many times did she say that to them? "Let me carry your cross." She helped so many carry a burden that wasn't hers to begin with and it took a toll on her, emotionally and physically. All she knew how to do was help those who didn't have the power to help themselves. Be the strength they didn't have. The group she'd created wasn't as strong as they used to be, especially since evil was more powerful now than it ever had been.

A tractor-trailer drove by and sounded its horn, knocking Sage back into reality. She thought better of calling to check in again. She grabbed her bag and headed to one of the picnic tables. Glancing around, she noticed that the little girl was still looking curiously her way. Sage smiled but turned her back and sat at the picnic table. She pulled a map out and spread it on the table. Taking off her necklace, she murmured, "Let's see how lucky I am today."

Sage held up the necklace and tried to scry to see if her father's location would show up. She tried a couple of times without getting any results. "Damn. Why aren't you showing up?" she muttered. "I have to be doing something wrong, or you're hiding just that well. Either way, Father, I will find you." She folded up the map and stuck it back into her bag.

"You will never find him if you keep using that sorcery," a voice near her said. Sage turned and saw a man sitting at the picnic table next to her. He was very average-looking, someone that wouldn't stand out in a crowd. He had wheat-blond hair that fell drably over his forehead. His clothes said he was nothing special. He sat with a slight slouch and an open book in front of him.

"Excuse me?"

"Don't tell me you didn't hear me," he said and slowly got up. "You are not going to find him that way." He enunciated every word as he walked toward her.

Sage decided to play along. She had never had a conversation like this with anyone random. But something about him reminded her of someone's grandfather. "Really? Then how am I going to find him?"

"It's simple," he said, sitting down next to her. Sage leaned away from the man but didn't break eye contact. "Just pray," he said. "He still thinks that you do not have to go looking for him."

"So all I have to do is pray," she said with a smirk on her face. "That's all? Is this some kind of joke?"

"Yes," he said with a smile, laying a hand on her shoulder. If any-one else had touched her so suddenly, Sage would have pinned them and asked questions later. There was something about this man, though. She felt strangely at ease around him.

"Who are you?" she asked.

"Just someone who knows more about you than you think. Let's go someplace where we can talk." He motioned to the little girl who was watching them and then pointed up to one of the viewpoints at the rest stop. Without waiting for a reply, he stood and headed in that direction.

Unsure of why she trusted this stranger, Sage got up and followed. Once they reached the viewpoint, the man waited until he knew they were alone and then spoke. "He knows what you did back there. How you took out the evil ones to help your friend. It was good work."

"Who are you talking about?" Sage asked. A breeze blew a strand of hair across her forehead, and Sage suddenly felt calmed. It was as though she'd heard a voice whispering that everything was okay.

"Sage, He also says that you do not have to fight anymore. You have done the work that you were supposed to do."

"You know what? Going after my father is something that I need to do," she shot back.

"That is the answer He was hoping to hear. There is a war coming. We need all the help we can get. The world is not the same as it used to be. Evil has managed to get a stronghold. The people that He created have lost their way. They have gotten out of control and do not know what is right and true. The values that were once held dear are gone. Those who are still good don't know how to fight. We need to help them. Help us and you will get to your father when the time is right."

"What?" Sage had this discussion in the past and it never ended well for either party. "The time to destroy him wasn't right when he was preparing to kill my mother?"

"No," he said. He reached out, as if to grab her hand, and then at the last second changed his mind. "I never said that. If you stay where you are and continue to search random haystacks who knows when you'll find him. Help us, and you will have some allies. There will be others who can make your life easier. Sage, you have made many enemies in your time here. Consider for a moment the benefit of a few friends."

Sage said, "I have fought plenty of the demons that walk this earth and the end result has always been the same. My team and I are still here. It doesn't matter how many more I'm going to have to destroy, or what side I have to play nice with. I'm not going to rest until I find the fallen angel that killed my mother."

"You mean your father."

"He lost that title a long time ago," she said as the anger began to build in her.

"What are you going to do when you do come face to face with him?"

"I'll do what should have been done a long time ago."

"Then what?" he asked. "When you have your revenge, then what are you going to do?"

"I'll worry about that when the time comes." She turned to make her way back to the picnic area.

The man caught up to her and grabbed her shoulder. Sage was surprised at his strength; it was more than any angel she had encountered before. "Just think about it," he said. "You cannot let revenge be the only thing that is keeping you here."

She looked at him, really studied his face, and realized that he was truly concerned about her. Worry lines had appeared on his forehead, and he still gripped her shoulder. "I'll think about it." She turned and walked down the path. When she reached the picnic area, she saw that the little girl was still watching her. "Do you need something, sweetie?" Sage asked her.

"No," she said. "I just wanted to tell you that two big goony-looking guys are over there, looking at your really cool bike."

The girl was right; two burly men with tattoos running up and down their arms were looking a little too closely at her bike. Sage looked at the girl with a smile.

"Watch this," she said. "I won't lay a hand on either of them, but they'll back off."

"O-okay," the girl said.

Sage walked over to the men and smiled, raising a brow. "Do you like what you see?" They turned and grinned back at Sage.

"Yeah," the first man said. He looked over to his buddy and the two of them took a step toward her. "What's a nice girl like you doing riding by herself?"

"Yeah," his buddy added in, following the other's lead. The second man was the smaller of the two. His greased-back hair and oily skin made Sage's stomach turn. "You should have some company, someone to protect you."

Sage couldn't tell if they were drunk or if this was their normal behavior. From the odor radiating off them, it seemed likely that they'd brushed their teeth with whiskey followed by a couple packs of cigarettes. She leaned back on the side of her bike, arms stretched out. Her left hand found the compartment where she stored her sword.

"You really want to know why I ride by myself? Why I don't have anyone to protect me?" She gripped the handle of the sword, shooting a wink over the men's shoulders to the girl standing at the edge of the parking lot.

"Of course, baby. I would love to ride with you," the first biker said. His grin widened, revealing a missing tooth.

"Good," she said with a grin. With a flick of her pointer finger, she unlocked the sword and pulled it out of its sheath so the blade glinted in the sun. She might as well have slapped the grins right off their faces.

"On second thought," the second man said, backing away, trying not to trip over his own feet, "maybe we should get going."

"Yeah, we don't want any trouble," the first man added as he joined his friend. Sage heard the little girl's laugh from across the parking lot.

"Thanks. I'm glad you realized that I have all the protection I need," Sage said, although the men were already rounding the corner. Sage pulled a small leather pouch out of her pack, reached in, and pulled out a small item. She walked over to the little girl who was still watching in awe. Sage felt connected to her. She wanted to do something for her.

"Thanks for helping me out there," Sage told her.

"You're welcome," the girl said, eyes shining.

"What's your name?"

"Sara."

"Well, Sara, normally you shouldn't take gifts from strangers. This time, though, I hope you'll make an exception. Here is a little gift for doing the right thing and helping me out." Sage handed Sara a small diamond. It was big enough for her to start a fund for college and hopefully make something of herself.

Sara took it and smiled. "Wow, thanks. It's really pretty. It has to be worth a lot of money." She held it up to the sun and watched as the light danced across the facets. "It sparkles, too." She turned and ran off to her parents.

Sage laughed. *So much for not taking gifts from strangers*, she thought. "Tell your parents you want a motorcycle, too," Sage called out after the girl. Sara waved good-bye as Sage climbed onto her bike.

A FEW HOURS later, Rowan and Hazel were driving down the same barren highway that Sage had been on. Hazel gazed mindlessly out the window. There was nothing interesting other than the occasional tractor-trailer speeding by.

They'd been on the road for a while, and the hours were passing in silence. Hazel fought boredom and the urge for sleep. She had only known Rowan for a short time, but her tough-girl attitude frightened Hazel a little. She fidgeted in her seat before making up her mind to strike up a conversation.

"How long have you been working with Sage?"

"Too long to remember. Why do you want to know?" Rowan's eyes never strayed from the road, and she held herself as though she had a steel spine.

"Just figured I would ask," Hazel said, putting her hands up. "It's a long drive and I figured it was as good a time as any to get to know each other better." Hazel knew Rowan had been alone for a long time, and it was clear she wasn't enjoying the opportunity to break in a new teammate. Rowan and Sage were still not over the death of their former partner, and Hazel hoped to somehow alleviate their pain. "So, where are you from?" Hazel drummed her fingers on her knees, and attempted to keep things light.

Rowan reached down and turned on the radio. Hazel sighed, sat back against the seat, and resumed her position gazing out the window. When a pop song came on the station she started humming quietly along. Out of the corner of her eye she saw Rowan cringe and flick the radio off once more.

"How about I ask you a question?" Rowan said.

"Sure, why not." Hazel sat up.

"Where did the name come from?" Rowan asked, settling in for a long backstory.

Hazel responded quickly, with pride. "It's my Grandmother's name. My mother named me for her." Silence fell, and Rowan rolled her eyes.

"Oh."

"I-I know it's not cool like yours, but it's mine and I'm happy with it," Hazel said, shrugging.

"We're just going to have to give you a nickname, since calling you Hazel is going to drive me nuts. I keep thinking I'm calling some old lady."

"Hey, a nickname? Cool!" She didn't respond to the old lady comment, though it stung. "What about Skye?"

Rowan grimaced and remained silent.

Hazel laughed and said, "Okay, not Skye. You think I'm stupid."

"I never said that."

"You didn't have to. I can tell. I'm the psychic one, remember?" Hazel fired back.

"Fine. You're right. I hated it, but I'm also tired so let's stop talking about it." The twitch of her lips belied her sharp tone.

"How about Shane?" Hazel looked up from some files she was looking through.

"No," Rowan said, never taking her eyes off the road, a grin now appearing on her face in full form.

"Feather?"

"No way."

"Buffy?"

"Taken." Rowan looked at Hazel and raised an eyebrow.

"Lilly?"

"Wonder if Sage will care if I leave you at the next rest stop," Rowan muttered.

"What?"

"Look, just give it a rest. When the time is right, the name will come to you. Until then just relax. Besides you can't give yourself a nickname. That's just not right."

Hazel settled back against her seat. "Thanks. So how long have you been working with Sage?"

"Too long to keep track. We have traveled so many roads together and have seen so many things that I stopped counting the years a while back."

"Why are you still here then?" Hazel asked.

"You mean, did Sage help carry my cross long enough so I could get closure?"

"Well, yes, did you? Get closure?"

"We took care of that a long time ago," Rowan said with a smile. "It was a release that I will never forget."

"Do you mind talking about it?" Suddenly Hazel felt unsure of herself. Perhaps it was too early to hear something so personal of her partner.

Rowan was quiet and Hazel wondered if she had pushed too far. She was about to apologize when Rowan spoke.

"It was my fiancé," she said. "We were a couple days from our wedding when he was killed. By a vampire."

They sat in silence for a few moments after this revelation. Hazel glanced at Rowan and whispered, "I'm sorry." Rowan looked out the window into darkness but Hazel knew where she really was.

"It's okay. It's all in the past. You find a way to move on and do what you need to make sure the goal is achieved. You survive."

"What made you stay?"

"I lost everything. I had nothing to go back to. When it really gets down to it, Sage and I became family. I saw Sage and knew there was no one watching her back. Neither of us had anyone to fall back on. I took the job and decided to stay for the long haul. Right now, Sage is the only family I have, and if you asked her, she would say the same thing for me. We are going to be standing together at the very end."

"Wow," Hazel said. "When do you think that is going to happen?"

"It will be sooner rather than later. There is something different in the air these days. I just want to make sure that I am on the right side when the battle goes down."

Hazel opened her mouth to ask what Rowan meant when her phone dinged. "It's Sage; she's telling us where to meet up with her." She held the phone up for Rowan to see.

"Well then I guess we better get going," Rowan said as Hazel entered the coordinates into the GPS.

"We're going to Ohio," Hazel said. "I heard there wasn't anything out there."

Rowan looked at the GPS and shook her head, "That may be true, but trust me. Sage knows where to go to find what she's looking for, and we don't want to keep her waiting."

FOUR

age pulled into the town Thomas called home. It was a college town on a Friday night, so there was a lot of action going on. There were school colors flying everywhere, rivals trash-talking people from the opposing team. Sage still couldn't get over the fact that Thomas had made this place his home for the last seven years. She parked her bike and looked around. Up and down the street there were packs of men and women heading—she could only assume—to the many bars in town. *Then again,* she thought, *he probably fits in perfectly around here.*

She had been here before and was familiar with the area. She was also adept at fitting into a crowd. If someone were to give her a quick look she would have passed as a graduate student looking to head out and have some fun, not someone searching for a vampire that was asking for her help.

She scanned the crowds, looking for anything that would tell her she was headed in the right direction. She passed a group of teenagers wearing dark clothing, all of them sporting spiky black hair and wearing eyeliner. She almost laughed. This group attempted desperately to portray something dark yet never came close to that goal. They made her feel old.

She turned a corner and saw the line to get into a loud, bright bar on the corner of the street, and her gut told her that was where she'd find him. She had known Thomas for a long time and knew what kind of person he was. He had been young when he was turned; he'd been a good-looking man. He knew how to use that to his advantage. She got in line and waited, watching the crowd and knowing this was exactly up Thomas's alley. They were young and not well seasoned. They were searching for any kind of attention. When she reached the entrance, she looked inside. It was certainly the type of scene where she might find Thomas. She tried not to laugh as she saw what looked like a beach club complete with lifeguard chairs, cabanas, and the smell of suntan lotion mixed with beer and sweat.

After a few minutes of getting sloshed with beer and getting hit on several times, the hairs on the back of her neck stood up. She felt as if someone was watching her.

"Maybe my luck is going to change," she said as she turned toward the only person who would be staring at her in this place. Thomas was walking across the room toward her, maintaining eye contact the entire way. There wasn't an ugliness to him like the typical male vampire. He was built like an athlete, but he also had a rough edge. Over the years Sage had gotten to know Thomas's history a little better. Thomas was born with a silver spoon in his mouth, but after some bad decisions he was cut off from the family. He had found a way to maintain the extravagant lifestyle he had been leading by getting a mentor who was a vampire. Last time she'd checked, he was the right-hand man to the vampire who was one of the elder family heads, so he knew what was going on in this town. Over the years he started to hate what the elders represented so had no problem voicing his opinion when things started to change.

"I figured all I had to do was go to the bar that had the most jail bait to find you," she said with a grin. He was, in some ways, an old friend, but he had a way of pushing Sage's buttons. She had the occasional urge to strangle him. He enjoyed being a vampire a little too much. There were different types of vampires, and Thomas was one who often rubbed Sage the wrong way.

"Nice to see you, too, sweets," he said with a smile that could have melted the hearts of the majority of the female demographic in the bar. "I see you got my texts. Believe me, I would much rather see you under friendlier circumstances, but I have a situation going on and could use some assistance. You were the only one I thought could help."

"Why should I help you?" Sage asked. Something was bothering her about this conversation. Thomas had a way of spinning things in his favor. She didn't want to get caught up in his old game.

Thomas scoped out the room and looked back to Sage. "Simple: a way to pay me back for all the favors that I've done for you. Besides, I haven't seen any Nephilim or fallen angels around here in a while—other than the new vampire queen."

"Vampire queen?"

"Yeah. A few weeks ago, this young woman came into the yearly Clan Summit and took over."

Sage knew there was only one way to do that. "You mean she killed off all those elders?"

"Yes. I was there. It was an absolute bloodbath."

"The only way a young vampire could do something like that is if they weren't just a vampire," Sage said.

"This is vampire territory. I know I haven't been the most support-ive of the old way, but what the new queen is doing is going to get us all killed." Thomas's eyes wandered to the door where a few women had just entered. They were young, blonde, and sported the latest in college gear. Thomas smiled in their direction. Sage smacked him on the shoulder to bring his focus back to her.

"You are just as bad as some of these horny frat boys. Are the jailbait still serving their purpose?"

"Still looking like I could pass for some of the younger ones around here."

"All right, let's focus on one thing at a time. First, why you called me." She wondered if she could find an excuse to make a quick exit.

"Can I at least buy you a drink?" he asked, still watching the women out of the corner of his eye.

Sage started toward the bar. "Can't say no to that."

"Good," Thomas said with a sly grin. "I was hoping you would say that." They finally got to the bar and Sage turned and smacked Thomas on the shoulder again.

Thomas's eyes widened. "What was that for?"

"Put your eyes back in their sockets and wipe the drool off your fangs. I felt your eyes checking out my backside all the way over here. I'd be surprised if I wasn't already undressed in that sick, twisted little head of yours."

"Oh, you are, but I still think that the real thing would be so much better," Thomas teased.

"I have told you, more than once: you are not my type."

The bartender, smiling at Sage, asked, "What will you guys have?"

"A double shot of Jack and Coke," Sage said, looking the man up and down and smiling back.

"I see you still like the whiskey," Thomas whispered into Sage's ear. "Who needs to put their eyes back in their sockets now?" He glanced at the bartender. "Give me whatever is good on tap."

"You trying to watch your figure or something?"

"I'd rather have a nice cognac, but when in Rome you've got to act like them so you can fit in."

"Damn, you might as well go full out and start taking some classes," Sage said.

"I could pull it off. I mean I'm a little over a hundred years old, and I still like this." He sat back on his stool. Sage watched him. His eyes continuously scanned the room. She wondered if he was looking for a girl to hit on or searching for something else.

"A hundred," Sage said sarcastically. The bartender came back with the drinks and Thomas told him to put it on his tab.

"After the first two hundred, age really doesn't matter anymore, or at least that's what the elders say. That's why it's fine to let yourself go." Thomas took a drink of beer. He immediately turned and spit it out into an empty glass sitting on the bar. Sage laughed as Thomas looked at the drinks in front of him. "How in the world anyone drinks this garbage is beyond me."

Sage grabbed her drink and downed it. Thomas watched her with a raised eyebrow. "You know you actually look like you fit in here better than I do." He asked the bartender for a different drink. "You still haven't told me what your type of guy is."

Sage laughed. "First, he has to be living."

"You know I heard once you go undead you never go back."

Sage snorted. "You know, I will give you credit, you have one twisted sense of humor."

"Well, making you laugh is a start. A small one but it's something."

Sage held up her glass, feeling more relaxed every second. "I'll drink to that."

Thomas put down his drink. "Now before we get down to business, how's the search going for the old man?"

"I haven't had a hint of where he might be since he broke out of Hell's Gate. The bastard is driving me nuts. I'm just hoping that I didn't lose his trail." Thomas was one of the few people Sage knew that actually understood.

"I know he's your father and that should make it easier to find him. But he's still a fallen angel."

Sage knew he was right, and maybe this was the reminder she needed to change her approach on how to look for him. "So you're saying I need to look at him differently. I need to look at him as just another bad guy that I'm hunting." Sage was surprised at how willing Thomas was to share some of the insight he'd gained over the years, but she wasn't about to interrupt him.

"You need to look for what he is: very old and very smart. He's managed to go off the grid for some time now. That means he is either on to you, or he just doesn't want to be found by anyone. Some bad stuff could be heading your way. The hunter could easily become the hunted."

"Tell me something I don't know." Sage took another drink. "There has always been something or someone hunting me ever since I could remember."

It was one of those rare occasions that Sage was caught off guard as Thomas took her hand and pulled her close. She felt the coldness of his hand wrapped around hers as he spoke. "If you let me, Sage, I could make this all better for you."

Sage pulled her hand away. "Forget it. I don't need you." Sage shot down the rest of her drink and got ready to leave. Perhaps this was just another one of Thomas's games.

"You can't blame a guy for trying," he said as he tried to catch up to Sage, who was already out the door.

"Thanks for the drink, Thomas." Sage wrapped the conversation up. She never liked to end a conversation on a bad note. "But you haven't even told me what I am doing here. I'm thinking this is just another of your games to try to get into my pants. I really don't think I'm going to be able to help you. If I get the team involved that means Rowan, and we know how she feels about your kind. I'll get your drink next time."

"There's some real trouble brewing here. I can really use your help."

Sage caught him giving that smile he was known for. He was fine. He would turn around and find some young girl to flirt with. "Take it easy, Thomas."

"You too, Sage." He had to let her go; it was time for the next part of the plan. He needed to show her that some real trouble was going on in the city. "Be careful. There are plenty of bad people around. Some of them wouldn't mind seeing you dead."

"I know," Sage said, showing the confidence that had gotten her this far in life in one piece. "And I am always careful." Sage headed back to her bike while Thomas went back into the bar.

Sage drove off. After a few minutes, four other motorcycles appeared behind her: two choppers and two racing bikes. The bikers caught up to her and Sage noticed that there were two men and two women. They surrounded Sage and forced her off the road to a rundown empty lot off the main drag.

"There's no reason for you to be around here." One of the females spoke first. She had short black hair and a tall figure, dressed all in leather. There was a piercing in her right eyebrow and bottom lip. She was quite obviously a vampire. "There are no fallen angels for you to hunt around here. You need to turn your pretty little head around and head out of here."

"That is, unless you've gotten the sudden urge to die," one of the male vampires added. He wore a denim vest and looked like he was part of a biker gang. There was nothing pretty about any of these vampires and they didn't let that bother them.

"If that is the case we would be more than happy to oblige," the second male vampire said. All four vampires surrounded Sage and pulled out their weapons, which were bladed in one fashion or another.

"Whoa, guys, that was really tough and everything," Sage said as she got off her bike. "Especially the whole 'that is unless you want to die' line. What is that, from a movie or something? I'm not looking for any trouble. I was just paying a visit to an old friend, and now I'll be on my way." Cautiously, Sage moved her hand to the compartment on her bike, which held her sword. Just as she grasped the handle, another motorcycle pulled up beside the group with a strange shape draped over the back. As the driver stood up, Sage realized that it was another vampire, and the odd shape was Thomas. The man pushed Thomas off the bike at Sage's feet then drove away. Thomas rolled over and he was bloodied and beaten. A knot formed in her stomach. This was her fault.

Thomas did his best to smile. "Sorry, sweets. Couldn't stay away from you. I said it was dangerous."

"So this was whom you came to talk to," the second female vampire accused Sage, punctuated by a kick to the ribs for Thomas.

As a vampire, Thomas would heal quickly, but it still didn't look good. "Come on, guys. You didn't have to do that. You know who I am and what I have done in the past. Whatever vendettas you have against me, leave Thomas out of it."

"That's not what the others would think. This man is an enemy to us, and the fact that he was talking with you just made you our enemy, too," the first female vampire said. "But you are right, we do know who you are as well as what you have done to our kind." She stopped for a moment and then looked to the others. "I'm sorry, I've been remiss in my manners. You should know the names of your killers."

Sage looked at her in surprise. "A polite vampire?"

"Yes," she said. "Not all of us are as barbaric as you. My name is Miriam." She gestured to the others.

"I am Jillian," said the woman with the long red hair, looking at Miriam like she was crazy. "These two guys are Frankie and Chuck."

Chuck looked back at her. "I said my name is Fang now." Frankie hit him in the arm, and Jillian just shook her head.

"We are not going to call you that, Chuck. Now, let's stick to the plan," Miriam said.

Sage was getting angry with her company. "Will you stop the tough act? It doesn't work for you. Why is Thomas your enemy?"

Frankie glanced down at Thomas. "That's irrelevant; you will both be destroyed by the time we are done with you."

Sage attempted to watch all the vampires at once, debating what her best move was. "Is that supposed to scare me?"

"No, but this will," Chuck said. He charged toward Sage, swinging a long sword at her. At the last second, Sage pulled her own sword out and rolled out of the way, swinging her weapon up in time to deflect the attack. While she was vulnerable on the ground, the other vampires followed suit, attacking.

Sage sprang up and leaped behind her bike. Her attackers changed direction and were almost upon her. In a matter of seconds, she had run through a list of possible outcomes in her head and then let her instincts take over. She grabbed a handful of dirt and threw it into the faces of all four vampires. Without pausing she followed that up with an attack of her own. The vampires swung blindly, trying to defend themselves as Sage jumped over her bike and swung. She took a nice chunk out of Frankie's right arm.

Jillian scrubbed at her eyes furiously. "Tell us, Sage. How do you plan on getting out of this one?"

"I'll keep fighting until the rest of my plan comes into focus," Sage said and launched another attack, trying not to overdo it. It was four on one. Sage had been in fights like this and knew that she couldn't try too much too fast, otherwise she was going to tire herself out and make a mistake. She just had to keep Thomas safe until he could join her. Or better yet, until the cavalry arrived.

"I knew you c-cared about me," Thomas said, wheezing slightly. There was a sheen of sweat on his face, but his color was looking better by the minute. The other vampires tried to make their way over to him to keep him down, but Sage did what she could to keep them occupied.

"Shut up, Thomas. You really pissed these guys off."

"Don't worry about me." He got up, pulling a Hanwei short ax from inside his jacket. "Just look after yourself," Thomas said, jumping into battle.

Sage looked at Thomas between swings. "Finally decided to join in?" The fight raged on, and with four on two, the vampires were the aggressors. Thomas and Sage had never fought together, which meant they had no idea how the other thought. Thomas's military style didn't blend well with the fluidity that came from Sage's years of martial arts training from masters. They burned unnecessary energy. Four on two was still rough odds for some trained fighters. A familiar truck came flying into the lot, horn blaring. Relief flooded Sage as she saw Rowan and Hazel.

Rowan looked over to Hazel and yelled, "Stay here, and I'll go help Sage." She scanned the scene and moved into attack mode. She charged and undid the two sai knives strapped to her legs. She was built like a warrior but had a grace that belied her tough exterior. Rowan leaped into the fray, breaking up the circle that surrounded Sage and Thomas.

"I thought you guys would be here sooner. I had it all set up for you to make a grand entrance, and you blew it," Sage said with a grin.

"Traffic sucked. And how many times have I told you not to set us up like that? If it wasn't for the tracking device Hazel put on your bike, we wouldn't have shown up at all." Rowan lifted her nose and took a deep breath. "Bloodsuckers! Why didn't you tell me we were fighting vampires?"

"Does it look like I had the chance? There are four of them. I was lucky Thomas finally decided to join the fight."

Rowan looked over to Thomas, who was fighting Jillian. "No way. A vampire helping non-vampires fight? Isn't that against some code or something?"

Sage and Rowan quickly fell into sync. Rowan was trained in similar styles as Sage, and Sage had taught Rowan a thing or two. They took on three of the vampires and managed to keep them guessing. Thomas took on the other vampire, swinging his ax deliberately, never wasting energy on a shot that would fall short. When he wasn't actually striking skin, he was making the vampire step backward to avoid being hit. In no time he had Jillian cornered.

Hazel watched the fighting, trying to figure out what she could do to help. She lacked basic fighting skills, but she couldn't just wait in the truck. Jillian spun wildly and kicked Thomas in the chest, sending him flying backward, his ax flying out of reach. Acting on instinct, Hazel ran over to the side of the truck and picked up some heavy rocks. She began tossing them at the vampires attacking her friends. Her aim was slightly off at first; it was difficult to judge where to throw when they were all moving around so much. Finally, though, she threw a rock that hit Jillian in the head. Hazel let out a cheer that ended abruptly when Jillian turned toward her.

"You had to resort to throwing rocks?" she shouted. Her only answer was another rock from Hazel right between the eyes. It staggered her and gave Hazel the opportunity to go in and help Thomas.

"Hi, I'm Hazel," she said and knelt down as she caught her breath. "Let me help you."

"Thomas," he said, extending a hand. "I'm glad to see you. Nice aim, by the way."

"Thanks. It was the only thing I could think of. Okay, let's get you out of here." She grabbed him by the shoulders and tried to pull him up. After about ten seconds of pure struggle with no progress, Hazel heaved a sigh. "This isn't going to work."

"I would say not." Thomas rubbed his hand over his mouth, and Hazel suspected he was attempting to cover a smile.

Hazel cast around for anything that could help. She caught sight of Sage and Rowan. "You think I could get any help over here?"

Sage barely glanced over. "Sorry, but I'm kind of busy right now."

"Besides," Rowan added, "the guy's a bloodsucker. He should be all healed up right about now."

Hazel looked down at Thomas. "Is that true?"

"I'm sorry, darling, you just looked so determined to do it on your own. I had to let you try."

"Jerk," said Hazel. Covering a smile of her own, she gently kicked him in the side.

"What was that for?" Thomas demanded. "That's the second time tonight I've been kicked in the ribs."

"It was for making me work when I didn't have to. Get up before I kick you somewhere else." Hazel reached out and helped him up.

"Thanks," Thomas said.

"Let's get out of here." They made a break back to the truck, Thomas leaning heavily on Hazel. The attacks continued, although Sage and Rowan were gaining the advantage. Two against three was much more their style. They worked in sync, anticipating each other's moves, blocking attacks as the other one recovered, spinning around, back to back. Their opponents were flustered by their teamwork. Chuck stepped backward and slipped up. Sage took the opportunity to push forward and bring her sword down in a flashing arc. Chuck's head soared away from his body. Both of the vampires fighting Rowan paused for a moment, looking at the head of their friend, which had rolled across their feet. Taking advantage of the distraction, Rowan twisted her sai in Miriam's chest.

"I haven't had this much fun in a while," Rowan said to Sage with a smile, dodging an attack from Frankie. "Why don't we fight vampires more often?" She quickly countered the attack with another sai shot to the heart. Sage finished the job with another beheading. Jillian, who had recovered from Hazel's meager attack, stood frozen for a moment and noticed the advantage was no longer hers as Frankie's head rolled toward her. She glanced at her bike, which was parked behind Sage and Rowan. Panic filling her eyes, she turned and ran off into the woods.

"That's right. Run, you leech," Rowan said. Sage saw an opportunity to test the new modifications on her weapon, the Angel's Wings. The weapon was primarily made for close-combat fights, but with the modifications she had made, the whole dynamic was changed.

"Check this out," Sage said then threw the blades at the fleeing vampire. Jillian dropped almost immediately after the weapon left Sage's hands.

"Wow." Rowan held her hand up for a high five. "Nice shot."

Thomas looked over to Hazel and whispered from the security of the truck, "Remind me never to make her angry."

"Not a problem. That was really good."

"Thanks for the save," Thomas called out as Sage and Rowan made their way over to the truck. He scrunched up his nose as they drew nearer and then looked toward Rowan. "I knew there was something different about you, but I couldn't figure it out until now." Rowan scowled.

Sage stepped between them. "All right, let's go back to our corners." A roar of motorcycles in the distance drowned out Sage's words. She stepped closer to the truck and shouted, "We don't have a lot of time before the next wave gets here."

Rowan looked to Sage and smiled, wiping the blood off her knives. "But I'm just about warmed up." Everybody looked up when they heard a single motorcycle. It was just pulling into the lot with them.

"It looks like we already have company," said Hazel.

A man who was well over six feet tall got off the bike. His hair was fiery red, and his eyes seemed to burn as well. As he walked toward them, his trench coat fluttered open, revealing copper chain mail underneath as well as a golden belt. Rowan tensed for attack.

Sage stepped in front of Rowan. "Stand down, he's on our side."

Rowan returned her sais to their place at her belt and watched Sage approach the man. He nodded at Sage. "It's been a long time." His voice demanded respect and he cut an impressive figure in his trench coat.

"Of all the people to show up," Sage said, relieved. "I wouldn't have expected you, Uriel."

"The time of war is upon us. Dark and evil are trying to make a move, and we were sent to help stop it. You need to get them—" Uriel gestured toward the group behind Sage. "—Out of here. I will take care of this."

Sage knew she had no choice in the matter. She had some pull in her line of work, but when an archangel gave an order, she was obliged to obey. "I understand. How will you take them out?"

Uriel smiled and reached an arm over his shoulder, pulling out a long bow. "With this—they won't know what hit them."

"I would love to see it," Sage said. She had seen an archangel in a fight only once, and she would take any opportunity to see it again.

"Not tonight," Uriel told her. "Make sure your friends are safe. The group coming is much bigger than the group you just fought. Now go. I can handle it." Without a word of argument, Sage turned back to the others.

"Is that who I think?" Hazel asked curiously.

"Uriel," Sage said nonchalantly. "Yeah, except we were told to go."

Rowan looked upset. "No, come on. I wanted to take the walking dead on myself. Sage, you and I could have taken them easily." She looked over to Uriel, who was getting his bow ready. "Thanks a lot. You just wanted target practice, didn't you?" Uriel waved at Rowan.

Hazel pulled on her arm and said, "You know he could kill you in the blink of an eye, right?"

"He wouldn't do that," Rowan said with a smirk. "Then he would have to do more of the dirty work himself. He needs us and he knows it."

"Don't push it." Sage got back on her bike. They heard Uriel's motorcycle start up and he took off to go after the second wave of motorcycle-riding vampires headed their way. Sage looked over to Thomas. "You need to tell me what in the hell is going on here, now."

"Right now a vampire named Meditrina has taken over. In one month she has managed to put herself in control of one of the clans and has eliminated all the other clan leaders in one night."

"Now she controls everything?" Hazel asked.

"She has made herself the queen," Thomas finished.

"What makes her different than all the other clan heads?" Rowan asked, her eyes never leaving Thomas's.

"Because she's not just a vampire. Meditrina is also a fallen angel."

"Isn't Meditrina the Roman goddess of wine?" Hazel said.

"Yes," Thomas replied. "She goes with that name because she says that blood is her new wine, and her thirst for it is insatiable."

Rowan said, "That's something you don't hear every day: a fallen angel that's taken on the characteristics of the undead."

"And the fact that she's power hungry isn't bad enough," said Hazel. "What would happen if this gets out?"

"Every Nephilim and fallen angel that is looking for some power will be trying to take out vampires and we will have a race war on our hands," said Rowan.

"And we were just told the end of days' battle has begun," Sage added in. "I think we all know what we have to do. Thomas, why were they after you?"

"I'm working with a small but strong group of vampires that oppose her rule. I was never really well liked but by siding with them my list of enemies grew tenfold."

"But why oppose her?" Rowan asked.

Thomas looked straight at Rowan, and she cast her eyes away from his intense gaze. "I had been working for one of the clan heads. I saw what Meditrina was capable of doing. I didn't agree with her unifying the clans and how she went about doing it. We had been able to exist in this city without being noticed before she came."

"Sure, you were unnoticed. With the exception of those you killed. I imagine they noticed you."

"Enough, Rowan," Sage said.

Thomas continued as though he hadn't heard her. "Our existence is threatened by Meditrina's quest for power. We decided it was time it stopped. A few of us started to fight back, and now we are on the verge of a war.

"Then there would be less of you blood ghouls around. Always a silver lining," shot Rowan.

"Rowan, isn't it time for you to start gathering any of the old jewelry you can off the bodies so we can get out of here tomorrow? Sydney is in need of a new shipment."

Rowan was almost snarling. "Not a bad idea. I could use some cleaner air to breathe. Besides, I saw some good stuff on one of the ones I stabbed through the heart." The last part was directed at Thomas, who Rowan knocked against as she strode toward the dead vampires.

"What is she doing with those vampires that you guys finished off? And who is Sydney?" Hazel asked.

"Hazel, there are a lot of things that you will learn in due time, but right now I need you to jump on the computer and start getting all the information you can about this Meditrina."

"Sure thing, boss." She climbed into the truck and pulled out her laptop.

"What's she planning to do, just hop on Google and see what comes up?" said Thomas.

"Not exactly," Sage said. "Over the many years I've been doing this, I built quite the extensive library on the supernatural underworld."

"That is impressive," Thomas said, breaking his gaze from Hazel. "It's good to see that you have evolved with the times."

"I've had to. The amount of journals I've kept over the years managed to take up a lot of space and made traveling difficult."

Hazel poked her head out the window. "I would love to see them sometime."

"Believe me, you will," Sage said. "Now get back to work." She smiled and turned back to Thomas. "What you need to do now is head back and tell the others to get ready. If Meditrina is as powerful as you say she is, we are going to have hell to pay. Tell them we need to have a plan on how to eliminate her."

"So you're offering to help?" Thomas asked.

"I have my own agenda."

Thomas gestured to Rowan. "What about her?" Thomas had known Rowan as long as he'd known Sage, and from the beginning they'd rubbed each other the wrong way.

"I'll take care of her. She won't pass on the opportunity to take out a couple of vampire baddies that have potential to be real trouble. Especially to her kind."

"Good. The more help the merrier," said Thomas with a smile that greatly resembled a grimace.

"You'll be able to make it back okay?" Sage was already making her way back to the truck.

"I'll be fine," he said with a genuine smile this time. "Besides, what would the vampire community think if they saw me riding into town on the back of your bike?"

"You have a point." Thomas nodded once in her direction and then turned and walked off into the darkness. Sage stood next to the open passenger side window of the truck and said to Hazel, "I need you to follow me to where we're staying tonight."

Hazel stopped her frantic typing for a moment. "What about Rowan?"

"Don't worry about her. The items she is collecting need to be sent out."

"Sent where?"

Sage chuckled. "My accountant. I have to keep this operation running, and what better way to do it than with the pretty pieces that we gather from the bad guys. Say what you want about vampires, but they have a habit of keeping their treasure close to them."

"I get it. Take back what the bad guys probably stole anyway."

"It all goes back to museums and collectors, back to places where it should be seen." Shifting uncomfortably, Sage grasped for something else to talk about. She still wasn't ready for Hazel to know all the finer details of the operation. "Rowan will meet up with us when she's ready."

"What's this thing between Rowan and Thomas? Why did Thomas think she wouldn't want to work with him?" Hazel asked.

"That would be a question for Rowan. Come on, being out here in the open is giving me the creeps. Don't know what could be lurking out there in the shadows." Sage waved then hopped on her bike. Hazel cast a final look in Rowan's direction, pulled out of the lot, and followed Sage.

FIVE

A few hours later, Hazel was looking at the notes she'd put together. "Where do we begin with Meditrina?" she asked Sage. "Also, shouldn't we wait for Rowan? She might want to hear some of this as well."

"Let's just start from the beginning, and don't worry about Rowan. She treats all those she goes against the same way." Sage finished her pizza and sat down on the ratty motel room chair.

"All right." Hazel took a sip from her soda. "This supernatural Google is so cool."

Sage laughed. "Good to hear. Until we can get you trained and ready to fight, this is going to be your job with the team."

"First off," Hazel said once Sage had gotten settled, "it seems like Meditrina was one of the early fallen angels. I couldn't find out anything about her at first, because she went under a different name back then."

"So does that mean—"

"Yes. From what I can tell, Meditrina is from the big escape from Hell's Gate."

"It seems I can finally start looking for my dad."

"How so?"

"If she was one of the fallen that escaped with my father, find her and I might get a little closer to finding him."

"Makes sense."

Sage's mind was racing. "Does it say how she managed to get her way in to the circle of vampires?"

Hazel looked at her notes. "My guess is it was the Blood Summit."

"The Blood Summit?"

"I thought it needed a name." Hazel looked a little embarrassed.

"Not bad," Sage told her. "I like it."

"How hard would it be to turn an angel into a vampire?" Hazel asked, fascinated by the thought.

"When you look at it from a scientific standpoint, an angel is already dead. So they only have to drink the blood of another vampire."

"You have a massive problem on your hands."

"You got it."

Hazel looked back at her notes. "After Meditrina turned, she disappeared for a couple of weeks until the summit."

"My guess is she was trying to learn what she could do with her new set of powers."

"Why would she want to become a vampire?" Hazel asked. "Especially since she was already an angel."

"Power," Sage said. "A chance to have more control than you had before. A chance to be stronger than you have ever been. I look at the vampires as the Devil's version of the angels. They have their master to serve and the angels have theirs. Both of them have similar powers."

"Wow." Hazel paused for a moment. "That's something I'd never really thought about. But it makes total sense."

"The thing I'm having a hard time with is how she's managed work both powers to her benefit."

"I don't get it."

"Being an angel—even a fallen angel—is on the opposite side of the spectrum from being a vampire," Sage said. "When you have two polar opposites working together in one person, the results are usually bad. Somehow she managed to find a balance. This could change the whole game. Big time."

"How so?"

"Think about it," Sage said, moving closer. "If fallen angels find out that they can take on the powers of another species, what's stopping them from becoming a more aggressive and dangerous opponent?"

"Yeah. I get it. She needs to be stopped before her eclipse becomes the trigger that sets off a new wave of trouble."

"Eclipse," Sage said, intrigued by the name Hazel had given it. "Why did you call it that?"

Hazel began to sketch an eclipse as she spoke. "It's when the sun or moon moves in front of or behind the earth, blocking the sun's rays. When this happens it creates darkness. So, you have a beautiful thing like an angel—"

"She is still a fallen angel," Sage said.

"Regardless of what she is there is still a beauty to her. So when the other thing moves in front of it, you get darkness. Sometimes large and other times small. The vampire is Meditrina's darkness, so the angel has become eclipsed."

"That is pretty impressive," Sage said. "I could go with that."

"Thanks." Hazel smiled shyly.

The door to the hotel room slammed open. Sage leaped out of her chair and pulled out a knife, shoving Hazel behind her. Rowan strode purposefully into the room. The corner of her mouth quirked up when she saw Sage in her fighting stance. Sage dropped back into the chair when she saw that there was no danger.

"You didn't leave the key like we talked about," Rowan said, "so I had to rely on some old skills I hadn't had to use in a while." She held up some thin metal tools.

"You picked the lock," Hazel said.

"Yeah. Tricks like that came in handy in my younger years. I was never short of food. So do we have a plan to take out this woman yet?"

"Good to see you back with us, Rowan," Sage said.

"Were you collecting jewels this whole time?" Hazel asked.

"Just had to take care of some things."

"Care to elaborate on that?"

"Not at this time," Rowan said. "Besides, we have more pressing matters to take care of."

"So, everything is well?" Sage asked, hoping to divert an argument.

"Yes."

"Are you in?" Sage asked.

"Yes. This is the reason I joined up with you all those years ago."

"All right," Sage said. "How does this sound? Tomorrow, early in the day, we check out the area where we're going to have the meeting with Thomas's allies and get a lay of the land. Then tomorrow night, we'll see how Thomas and his merry band of bloodsuckers can behave themselves around us."

"A Vampire United Nations. Can't wait," Rowan said.

"Then from there?" Hazel was nervous about fighting without any real training. She knew conflict was inevitable, but she didn't expect her first mission to be this soon.

"We go on the attack, going after the objective like we always do," Sage said.

"Are you ready for your first fight?" Rowan asked Hazel.

"As ready as I'll ever be," Hazel answered and began biting her nails.

"That's the spirit, kid." Rowan smacked her on the back, knocking Hazel to the ground.

Sage headed over to her weapons to make sure they were clean and in working order. "Besides, Hazel, you'll be doing a lot of your work from the truck. You are going to be our eyes and ears for this."

"What's its name?" Hazel watched Sage prep her sword with as much precision and care as a jeweler creating a masterpiece.

"What?" Sage glanced up.

"The sword. Arthur had Excalibur. Charlemagne had Joyeuse. El Cid had Colada. All warriors have names for their sword. What's the name of yours?"

"This is Dragon's Claw. I have had this sword for as long as I can remember. It was made for me while I was in Japan a long time ago. They almost never make swords like this anymore. I was the first woman the smith ever made a sword for. It's called Dragon's Claw for this." Sage held out the sword, showing Hazel the pommel, which had a red-and-blue-jeweled claw embedded in it. The talons were an inch long.

"Wow," Hazel said. "Now that's vicious."

"It needs to be. I have to gut these Nephilim to truly stop them. Here, let me show you. Rowan, hold the pizza box up for me."

Sage pointed the blade down, claw toward the ceiling. She thrust it toward the pizza box, claws first. It went into the box, and Sage ripped the sword out, leaving behind a nasty, jagged hole.

"It still looks kind of awkward because of that claw," Hazel said.

Sage held the sword out on the side of her hand. "You see? Perfectly balanced. The man who made this for me knew the art of sword making. It is almost impossible to find a sword of this quality anymore."

"I see," Hazel said.

"I have another weapon to show you." She took a bronze metal circle off her belt and held it out to Hazel. There was an intricate design of swirls on the circle, like old writing.

"What's that?" Hazel asked.

"This is for when we are in a close quarters with those we're fighting, and there isn't enough room for Dragon's Claw."

Sage straightened, and Hazel stepped out of her way. Sage flicked her wrists, and the circle split into two. With another flick, the circles opened up and became a two-bladed weapon. "These are what I call my angel's wings. They are also designed by my Japanese friends. With a slight modification to the original design, they can be used as a throwing weapon like you saw earlier tonight."

"That is so cool. I'm glad we're not enemies," Hazel said. "What's your weapon of choice?" she asked Rowan.

Rowan held up two oddly shaped knives. "These are called sais. There's nothing really special about them. No big story. They were simply weapons that work with my style of fighting. I picked them up and they became extensions of my arms. I haven't really used anything else since. Don't get me wrong, I still keep other weapons nearby in case of an emergency." Rowan reached down the front of her shirt and pulled a small throwing dagger from between her breasts.

"That could come in handy. You two must have a hell of a time getting through airport security."

"True, but funny enough, no one ever asks to search us." Rowan grinned.

"I'm going to have to choose a weapon if I'm planning to hang with you girls."

"Don't worry," Sage said. "There will be plenty of time for that. Right now we need you to focus on the abilities that you do have. That has been missing from this team for a long time. Learning to defend yourself in combat will come when it needs to."

"But if you need them, there are plenty of weapons in the truck," Rowan added.

Sage said, "Enough about that. We need to ask for protection for tomorrow."

Rowan nodded and went off to a corner of the hotel room on her own. She grabbed her bag and settled down in her chair, turning it to face the window.

"Hey," Hazel said to Sage. "What is she doing?"

"Praying to those gods she believes in."

"Does it help her?"

"She does what she has to so she can sleep at night. I may not believe in the same gods, but it works for her."

"So what do you believe in?"

"I spend a lot of time reading." Sage tugged a book out of her bag and handed it to Hazel.

"The Bible," Hazel said. "If you're a Christian, and Rowan's a pagan, doesn't that mean you're not really supposed to work together?

That's what the churches always said and that's what turned me away from all religion."

"Yes, but a wise man once told me that the best way to be who we are is by being the brightest light we can be."

"I like that. I should probably leave you to do what you need."

"You are welcome to join me."

"No, thanks. Maybe next time. Right now I need some time to myself. There was a lot to take in today."

"I understand. When you're ready, I'm here. Oh, and Hazel? Don't be gone too long. You don't want to miss what else goes on before a potential confrontation."

Hazel opened her mouth to ask but seemed to change her mind. "I'll be back in a little while then."

After Hazel left, Sage closed her eyes in prayer. "All right, Father. You brought Hazel into the fold and I understand that this is your work. I know we haven't seen eye to eye on some things, but I ask you to protect and watch over her. She doesn't know enough yet. The world is dark and she is still an innocent light. Also, I can't lose another one."

SIX

fter Rowan and Sage finished with their prayers, and Hazel returned from her walk, they made their way to one of the rowdiest bars they could find for the second half of the pre-conflict ritual. The bar was the right combination of the college crowd and people that were just looking to let loose from their workweek. The room was pumping with energy when they walked in, and it smelled of sweat and beer. Sage and Hazel sat at the closest thing to a quiet table they could find, while Rowan wandered off toward the back.

"This is what you guys do before you go after the bad guys?" Hazel asked. She had spent her time in some bars when running around, but they were quiet compared to this place.

Sage grabbed a bottle of tequila and poured them both a shot. "This is sort of a tradition for Rowan and me. It's nice to have a third person back on the team. It makes this part a little more fun for me."

Hazel drank her shot and coughed at the alcohol's bite. It really wasn't her drink of choice, but she needed to fit in. "Why is that?"

Sage looked around the room. "Did you notice how quickly Rowan disappeared?" She took her shot with ease and slammed the empty glass down on the table. Hazel was beginning to wonder how Sage was going to function drinking the way she was. It didn't cross her mind that the alcohol might affect her, too.

"Rowan doesn't seem like the partying type," Hazel said. As if on cue, Rowan and two other girls jumped up onto the bar and started dancing for a crowd of onlookers. Sage applauded.

"The thing that makes it even funnier is that she is completely sober," Sage said, leaning over to Hazel.

Hazel watched for a moment in disbelief. "No way I would never be able to do something like that. I am way too shy."

Sage poured another shot. "With a couple more of these in you, you'll lose that 'blushing youth' thing pretty quickly."

"How are you so sure?"

"When you've been around as long as I have, you notice things that the average person doesn't even think about."

"You don't understand. I am intensely shy. I could never do some of the things that you guys have done."

"Don't tell me you heard what we did in that bar in Nashville. Or was it in Kazan?" She waved her hand, dismissing the thought. "We got a little too into our pre-fight rituals back then."

"Kazan, Russia? I need to hear this."

"Not tonight. Don't worry. In time, the three of us will have stories of our own to tell."

The song ended, and Rowan climbed off the bar. The girls tried to hug her, but she pulled away from them. She headed over to Sage and Hazel.

"Well, look who decided to join us," said Sage. "You know, Rowan, I think they really wanted hugs."

Rowan cast a disparaging look to Sage. "I don't do girly." She took a sip of water.

"Always remember that," Sage said to Hazel.

"She reminded me once already," Hazel replied.

Rowan pulled up a chair and sat with them. "This is how I get ready for a fight. I saw one of those ultimate fighting guys do the same thing and decided to try it. So, are you guys having fun?"

"We're having a great time watching you," Sage said.

"I never would have thought that you would be that good at danc-ing," Hazel said.

"All I'm doing is having some fun and letting off a little steam. It's the closest thing to meditating that keeps the adrenaline pumping."

Sage offered Rowan a shot. "Do you want a drink?"

"Sage, you know I never drink before a fight. It messes with my head too much. After a fight, well, that's another story." She handed the shot to Hazel, who reluctantly took it.

"All the more for us." Sage toasted Hazel and downed her shot.

"So do you guys want to come out and dance?" Rowan asked.

"I'm not the dancing type. Besides half of those people watching are thinking the same thing," said Hazel.

"As long as 'thinking' is all they're doing. If one of them tries some-thing, well, we know what happens."

"Kazan," Hazel said and laughed.

"You told her?" Rowan said to Sage.

"Nope," Sage said. "I told her something happened there. You gave her the rest. We've got ourselves quite the little detective here."

"I didn't tell her a thing," Rowan said, looking back to the dance floor. "Besides, he deserved what he got." Sage and Rowan laughed.

"Hazel," Rowan said. "Care to join me?"

"You know, why not?" She stood up and stumbled. Rowan and Sage each grabbed an arm to keep her from falling.

"Maybe you should sit this one out," Sage said as she helped Hazel sit back down.

"Not a big drinker, are you?" Rowan said.

Hazel opened her mouth and the words came out after a brief pause. "I really didn't think that I had that much."

Sage held up the three-quarters-empty bottle.

"Oh my, I guess I drank a little more than I thought." Hazel paused. "Why is the room spinning?"

Rowan got Hazel up on her feet. "I think it's time to go," she said to Sage.

"What's the matter?" Hazel asked.

"If we don't get you back to the hotel quickly enough, you're going to get sick in front of all these nice people."

"Let's get going then. But not too fast, or I will be sick."

MEDITRINA STOOD AND looked out the bay window to the night of the city below with a quiet confidence. She watched the people walking and the action of the night. "I can make this town mine," she said. She cut a sharp figure in her crimson red suit. Four vampires from her upper command entered the "war room," as Meditrina had affectionately nicknamed it. She made her way to the table, her red pumps echoing through the room with every long stride. She sat down in the high-back chair at the head of the table and looked at her chosen four. Two males and two females. They were dressed to fit in with a younger crowd. Nothing separated them from anyone else, with the exception of being unable to be in the direct sunlight.

There was a sixth spot at the table next to Meditrina, and that was for Thomas. She smiled as she thought of his special assignment. His absence could be forgiven. The room had changed somewhat since Meditrina's reign began. It had needed to move out of the old world and into the new. She had added a modern flare. Everything was sleeker. The table now had a glass center that doubled as a computer screen.

"It seems that we have several things to discuss tonight, so let's get right down to business," said Meditrina. "The time has come for the vampires to reestablish themselves as the dominant race." The four vampires nodded in unison. One of the women applauded the comment. "It's time for us to make a statement. October eleventh, we will have the Meditrinala. The celebration will take place in this building, our club. Then by the end of the night we will have taken over this town. We have seen the light fade.

Crime has gone up; the education system is horrible. The youth are looking for better and quicker answers. By the time this festival is done the light will be out of this town permanently." She spoke like a politician, slamming her fists onto the table for emphasis. With each bang from her fist, the other vampires jumped. Meditrina smiled. She had instilled enough fear in these minions that they would do whatever she wanted.

"How do we make this plan happen?" Alexei, one of the male vampires that rose quickly through Meditrina's new ranks, spoke up. He believed in the cause but he also wasn't trusting of anyone older than him. He thought the elders had put the clans in this situation. He wasn't going to let someone else do the same thing.

"We play with the human emotions." Meditrina leaned in. "We go after their desires. We spin a web of deceit and tell them exactly what they want to hear."

"How is this going to help us gain power?" He hesitated a moment before plowing on. "Meditrina, this sounds like a lot of smoke and mirrors. What if this whole plan of yours fails? Did you even tell them that Sage McKenzie is in town?"

"What?" said Caden, the second male vampire. He was an educated young vampire who had some understanding of the bigger picture. But he was also hungry to taste real power. Meditrina stood up, blood rushing to her face. They were challenging her. She tried to keep her wits about her and not let them see her anger. She walked over to the vampire that was instigating the whole thing.

"You are worried about my plan not working because of Sage McKenzie." She inched closer to his face. "It's so nice to hear you voice your concerns." She looked to the others that sat at the table. "All of you should voice your concerns," she said with a grin. Out of nowhere, Meditrina slit Alexei's throat like a surgeon making an incision. Blood poured down his neck as the body slumped forward onto the table. Meditrina grinned then brought the blade up to her mouth and licked it clean. "But in the future, know that I prefer you to have a little respect."

She walked to the back of the room and clapped her hands twice. A few servants rushed in to take care of the body. Meditrina looked at the remaining three vampires. "Damn, now I need to find someone to take his place. Anyone have any suggestions?"

"None, none at all," one of the women vampires said, followed by silence.

"Do we need to have any more discussions on how the festival will go?"

"No, Mistress."

"Now onto other things." Meditrina put her blade away and began to tap the keys on the laptop. A picture of Sage McKenzie appeared on the screen in the center of the table. Meditrina cringed at the sight of her. She knew this girl's history, and was surprised that Sage had waited this long to go after her. "This is Sage McKenzie, in case anyone has not been paying attention. Apparently her newest assignment is me."

"M-mistress?" Caden's voice trembled.

"Yes?" Meditrina said, enjoying his discomfort.

"How should we handle this situation?"

"I really don't want you to worry about that." She stood up abruptly—causing the vampires to sink further into their chairs—and walked toward the window. "I already have a plan in motion that will take care of her and her team one way or another. She is coming for me because she thinks I have information she wants."

"Do you?" one of the female vampires asked, almost before she realized what she was doing. "Maybe it would be wise to share that information with your council?"

"When the time comes, you will finally understand. Not a moment before. Is that clear?"

"Yes, Mistress," they responded together.

"Now, leave me." Meditrina smiled; she loved obedience. Especially when it came to the orders she gave. "There are other matters I need to take care of." She went back to looking out the window as the other vampires quickly exited the room.

SEVEN

Sage was polishing her sword in the hotel room when Rowan returned from her morning run. "Do you think we should wake up sleeping beauty?" Sage asked.

"She has been out for quite a while now," Rowan said. "I remember when that was me."

Sage stifled a laugh. "The kid was taking those shots pretty hard, and it was obvious she wasn't used to drinking like that."

"It was a pretty effective way to remind her that we are not like her," Rowan said as she stretched. "She needs to realize that we are going to react differently to certain things. But it was another good initiation for the new team member."

Right on cue, a moan came from the bedroom. "It lives." Rowan chuckled. After another moan, Hazel burst from the room and disappeared into the bathroom.

Sage laughed. "Here's hoping she makes it."

After a few moments, Hazel emerged from the bathroom. "Will someone please tell me how to make the room stop spinning?" Hazel said, her pale face covered in a sheen of sweat.

Rowan got up and pulled some orange juice and lime juice from the refrigerator. She pulled cumin powder out of her bag, mixed the contents together in a glass, and handed it to Hazel. "I got you a few things. Drink it. It will help."

Hazel looked unsure for a moment then shrugged and drank it in one swift move. She made a face as it went down then looked at Sage and asked, "How is it that you remained perfectly fine? We were going pretty heavy on those shots last night." Hazel dropped into a chair at the small table.

"It does help when you are not completely human," Sage said as she began to put her weapons away.

"I keep forgetting that."

"Sorry, kid, the same goes for me," Rowan said, heading to the bathroom.

"So you're the same as Sage?" Hazel called after her.

Rowan stopped for a moment but didn't turn around. "Not exactly." Silence followed her ambiguous statement, and Hazel was about to prompt her to continue when Sage spoke.

"It's okay, Rowan."

Rowan turned toward Hazel. "I am what you would call—" Sage's cell phone went off, making Hazel jump.

"Hello." Sage held the phone to her ear. She stood and walked into the other room.

"Sage, it's Thomas. The meeting is set up for tonight, which is a good thing. It sounds like Meditrina is planning a little party to welcome in her new reign of terror and the start of the vampire takeover."

"Good to hear, but why does she want to throw a party?"

"She's claiming to be the vampire incarnation of the goddess for whom she was named. She wants to bring a whole new view to the vampire species, and it begins by taking over this town. So it looks like she will be pulling out all the stops, and everyone will be invited. Convert them or eliminate them."

"That doesn't sound good." Sage knew a lot of blood would be spilled at this event, yet Thomas seemed distracted. "It doesn't seem like that's the only problem tonight. What else is going on in the vampire world?"

"The others aren't happy that you're offering your services. Heck, for all they know, you've probably killed some of their friends. They know all about you, especially your partner. They don't trust her one bit."

There was a good chance that Sage and Rowan had killed some of their friends. Sage glanced into the other room at Rowan. If anyone else had been looking, they would have seen two women chatting. Sage knew Rowan though, knew that the tilt of her head meant she was keeping one ear on Sage's telephone conversation.

"Do you want us to back off? You want to handle this on your own?" She already knew what the response would be. She wanted to give him the opportunity to back out of this whole thing and maintain his dignity.

"Of course not. You guys are probably the only chance we have to get at Meditrina. These vampires that disagree with her rule don't have a clue about fighting. All these years of peace between the tribes has made them soft. They are more like politicians than anything. What we need is a general, and you are the most qualified as far as I can see."

"It's settled, then," Sage responded.

"You're right," Thomas said. "We'll just have to convince the others that you and your little band aren't just going to help us out and then kill us when it's all over."

"Well, that shouldn't be too difficult." Sage saw the corner of Rowan's mouth quirk up and knew that Rowan was able to hear Thomas as well as Sage.

"What about Rowan? Once they get wind of what she is, we might have a problem. Plenty of vampires still have a hard time letting go of the battles between the two, though it would benefit all in the bigger picture."

"You have a point," Sage said. This wasn't her problem to solve. If these vampires couldn't fight their way out of a paper bag, then someone had to help them do it. Thomas had asked Sage, so he would have to figure out a way to make it happen without causing too much dissention in the vampire community. "You seem to trust her."

"I know what she is, and I don't like that. But she hasn't given me a reason not to trust her. So I'm taking a chance," Thomas said.

"Just remember, it's all of us or none of us. Are we joining you in this meeting or not?"

"Can I ever say no to you? I'll call you later with the details. I have some other things to tend to before it happens."

"Talk to you later. Bye." Sage joined Rowan and Hazel once more. Hazel was waiting to get caught up on the conversation.

"Who was that?" she asked.

"It was Thomas. As of right now the meeting is on, but we may have a problem. Some of these vamps think we won't play well together."

Rowan, who had been quiet through the whole thing, finally spoke up. "Don't these bastards realize that I am not like the rest of my kind? Don't they realize that we have a common enemy right now?"

"I know that, and I think that Thomas knows too. That's why you need to cut him some slack."

"But I don't like him one bit. Never have and I never will."

"Why is that?" Sage asked.

"He's so into you, I almost think he wants to turn you," Rowan said.

"He doesn't have a chance in hell of doing that."

"Are you trying to convince you or me?"

Sage stepped closer to Rowan. "You need to stand down, warrior. My loyalty lies with this team and the fight we agreed to fight together."

Hazel stood up, hands fluttering toward the two women shooting daggers at each other. "Rowan, you never finished telling me what you are."

Sage kept her eyes on Rowan for another moment before turning toward the bed where her suitcase lay half-packed. "It's almost time to check out. You know my rule. We never stay in a place for more than one night. We could easily become a target here."

"Fine," Hazel said, slowly standing up. She promptly lost her balance and sat down heavily. "On second thought, maybe I should sit just a little bit longer."

EIGHT

The team spent the day gathering all the information they could about the area and what they were getting themselves into. When night fell, the three women gathered their equipment and went to the warehouse district. The area had seen better days. The economy had taken its toll. Occasionally there were signs of life, but never anything of interest.

Sage took the lead on her bike. Rowan and Hazel were following behind in a new truck. They pulled into a parking lot and waited. Sage was gathering her things when Rowan and Hazel approached her bike.

"Tell me again how the trucks were switched," Hazel said.

"Sage has friends available to her whenever she needs them," Rowan said.

"And they prefer to work in the middle of the night?"

Rowan was silent for a moment, unsure how to answer.

Sage saved her the trouble. "If you were them you would prefer to work when there's no one around to notice, too."

"So how are we going to do this?" Hazel bounced from one foot to another nervously. "I have done some shady things before, but nothing like this."

"You mean you've never had a meeting with vampires before? My dear, you haven't lived." Sage said, a sparkle in her eyes.

"No." Hazel grinned.

"We're going to head down and see what this meeting is about." Rowan got straight to the point.

"You are going to stay back and monitor everything from the back of the truck," Sage added.

"The back of the truck." Hazel wasn't sure about the whole idea but it was going to be better than dealing with the vampires face to face. "But…"

Rowan laughed and led Hazel to the back. "Never judge a book by its cover, kid." Rowan opened the back of the truck to reveal several monitors and other electronics. Everything looked like top-of-the-line surveillance equipment. "This is how you're keeping an eye on us."

Hazel's eyes widened, and she stood frozen for a moment. "That's… no way. Most of this isn't even supposed to be out on the market yet."

"Don't worry," Sage said. She could appreciate Hazel's excitement. She would know exactly how to work all the equipment. "It's not. You are one of the only people to actually see this stuff. I have some connections that we don't need to discuss right now."

"Do you think you can handle this stuff?" Rowan asked, not sure if the equipment was too advanced for her.

Hazel didn't answer. She disappeared into the truck, flicking the machines on as passed them. She smiled like a kid in a toy store, ignoring how absurd that comment sounded to her. "I'll be fine. You guys get going." She handed Rowan and Sage communicators and then closed the door.

Sage glanced at Rowan as they made their way to the meeting and whispered, "Something just doesn't feel right."

Before Rowan could answer, the communicators crackled to life. "This is Mother Nature with your first radio check. Over."

Rowan held her communicator to her mouth. "All right 'Mother Nature.' We read you loud and clear."

"Great. I've always wanted to try that. But next time say 'over,' so I know when your sentence is over. Over," Hazel said.

"Just remember you are our eyes and ears out here. If you see anything even the slightest bit suspicious, you need to let us know." Sage paused for a moment and then rolled her eyes. "Over."

"Okay, good luck, guys. Over and out."

Rowan and Sage placed the communicators back on their belts and continued on as quietly as possible. After a few minutes, Rowan pointed ahead where there was small fire burning. Rowan smiled and two women picked up the pace. They continued to walk in silence, ready for anything. The communicator came crackling to life, taking them by surprise.

"Hey, Sage, just to start my education while we go a minute, what is the best way to kill a vampire?"

"Well," Sage said. There wasn't a lot of time for chitchat but Sage never had any issues teaching so she made it short and simple. "There are two ways to take them out, and it's the same for many supernatural beings we face. We take out the source of their power. We stop what makes them work, like taking the batteries out of a remote control."

"Wait, are you saying you either take out the heart or the brain? Yuck."

"With vampires, you usually just take off the head," Rowan added, trying to lessen the visual that Hazel had provided.

"How many vampires have you killed?" Hazel asked, feeling a little bit queasy.

"Hundreds," Sage said, going through the numbers in her head.

"And don't forget the other monsters as well," Rowan added in. "But neither of us really keep score.

"Don't worry, you will have your chance soon enough."

"Really?" Hazel asked. "There's no rush. So when you say that's the same for almost all supernatural creatures, does that include the both of you?"

Sage and Rowan looked at each other. Rowan said, "Yes. Yes that includes us."

"Okay," Hazel said. "I just needed to check. If I'm going to be part of the team I need to start learning about all this stuff. I figured it was a good thing to learn how to kill most of you."

"Oh just you wait. When we get going with your training I am going to show you one of my favorite ways to—"

Sage said, "All right, ladies, let's focus. Hazel, give me the lay of the land. And tell me about the others that we're meeting up with." The window for chatter was closed and it was heading into game time.

"We have contact about one hundred yards out. There is a group of them. It's hard to make out exactly how many of them but my guess would be about a dozen."

"What are they doing?" Rowan asked, straining to see as far ahead as possible.

"It looks like they're talking. Well, arguing would be more accurate."

"Thanks, Hazel. Rowan, let's go. We've got to get to them before they notice us."

Rowan picked up the pace to keep up with Sage and put her hand on her weapon. They walked in silence for a few more minutes. Hazel's hushed voice came over the communicator once again.

"Rowan, I was thinking?"

"Right now is not the best time to be chatting."

"How about Reign?"

"Let's not do this now," Rowan said, knowing she was still going to go on about it.

"Sapphire?"

"No."

"What is she doing?" Sage asked, confused but trying not to laugh at how crazy it was making Rowan.

"Bree?"

Rowan rolled her eyes. "Hazel, please." She glanced at Sage. "She's trying to come up with a nickname."

"Ciara."

"There is nothing the slightest bit dark about you."

Sage looked over to Rowan, impressed that she knew what the name meant. Rowan returned her gaze. "What?"

"Looks like you like her already," Sage responded with a grin.

Just as Rowan was about to respond, Thomas noticed them and jogged over. He was comfortable for the environment that he was in but his clothes still showed a level of high end. "Ladies," he said, trying to hide the frustration in his eyes. "I would be much friendlier, but right now I have a bit of a situation on my hands. My friends don't like you." This last comment was directed unabashedly toward Rowan.

She looked over to the crowd and smiled. "No wonder. I think we may have taken out a couple of their buddies." Rowan waved.

"Really, Rowan?" Sage frowned at her.

"What, can't I have a little bit of fun?"

"Not this time." Sage shook her head. "Thomas, let me talk to them. I have an idea. It may alienate some of them even more, but there's a chance it will help win the rest over.

"Okay," he said, "but wait until my signal."

Thomas walked over to the group of vampires and began to talk to them. Rowan kept her eyes on the group and her hand on her weapon. "Do you think this will work?"

"At this point we don't have a choice," Sage said as they watched four vampires get up and leave.

"I would rather go down fighting than have a werewolf help us out." One of the vampires spoke loudly as he walked away.

"Same goes for me," another vampire agreed.

"Well there goes some of them," Rowan said. "It's a shame they can't see that the only harm I intend to inflict is on Meditrina and her people."

"Those would have been the harder ones to convince anyway," Sage said.

Thomas waved them over. As they drew nearer, Thomas looked more and more uncomfortable. Before they reached the group, he held up a hand to stop them and pointed to Sage.

Hazel's voice crackled in their earpieces. "I don't like this one bit."

"Neither do I. Let's get out of here," said Rowan. She didn't like that they were about to work with vampires.

"No," Sage said, "we have no choice on this. I will say what I have to and then we will walk away. If they want to join up with us then they'll catch up before we leave." Without waiting for a response, Sage walked toward the group.

"Hazel," Rowan said. "Get the truck ready to roll. We may need to make a quick getaway."

"Understood. I will start it up now," Hazel said. She hit the remote starter but stayed locked in on the computers.

"Hazel, can you hear anything they're talking about?"

There was just silence for a few moments, and then Hazel cleared her throat. "Um. Yes. I can hear parts of it."

"Well, what are they saying?"

"They're not going to be your best friends anytime soon."

"What?"

"They aren't being very nice about you," Hazel said.

Rowan took a step forward but stopped when Sage turned and began making her way back.

"Come on. Let's head back to the truck and see what comes of this," Sage said and the two started walking away. Before they could make it too far, Hazel jumped back on the communicator.

"You won't believe this, but it looks like everyone just left."

"What do you mean?" Sage said.

"I don't see a single sign of their vehicles or them," Hazel said.

"It's sounding like they may have had some problems of their own."

"You may be right. I don't feel like taking any chances," Sage said. On cue, the two of them pulled out their weapons.

As they turned, they saw Thomas and two other vampires—a man and a woman—walking toward them. Thomas looked rough around the edges. The other vampires looked very different from Thomas. The female seemed to be the younger of the two, but how vampires looked had nothing to do with their physical ages. Her hair fell a little lower than her shoulders. Her eyes were as dark as slate, and a piercing glinted in her right eyebrow. Her clothes were modern, and she wore bits and pieces of a military uniform mixed with a few Goth pieces.

The man looked older. His eyes showed years of experience. He was a well-built African American, smartly dressed; the attire said he was a man of classic elegance. There was something strange about him, something that didn't fit.

Once the three got close enough that and Sage and Rowan could see whom they were, Thomas spoke up. "There's no need for any of that." He gestured to their drawn weapons. "We come here unarmed." The three vampires opened their jackets as proof of his statement.

Sage lowered her weapon and looked over to Rowan, who reluctantly did the same, before saying, "So what happened to the other band of bloodsuckers? Did they decide it was better to just run away?"

"No, they just didn't agree with some of the details in the little escapade," Thomas said to Rowan, never taking his eyes off her.

"What? We are about to take on a vampire that is giving all other vampires a bad name. Which, by the way, is not easy to do. She's hungry for power and will go to any length to get it. That's not important to them?"

"Sorry, sweetheart, but some of us only like to play with our own kind."

That set Rowan off. "So they are afraid to work with someone that is supposed to be their sworn enemy, but you aren't even the slightest bit afraid of me." She took a step toward Thomas, a vein beginning to show on her temple. When Rowan went into attack mode the two other vampires stepped toward her to show their support and protect Thomas.

Thomas motioned for the others to step back. "Some of them would consider it treason to be working with you."

"So what's your story? Why did you choose to stay?" Sage directed her question at the man and woman.

The female vampire stepped forward. "My name is Liberty. Meditrina needs to go down. That has to be the priority here. We have managed to find a place where we can all exist. We don't need to be worrying about humans hunting us down like it is a witch-hunt. All we want to do is exist on our own in peace and quiet."

Rowan snorted but collected herself and spoke. "I will agree with you on one thing. If Meditrina did gain enough power and continued the way she's going we would be looking at the extinction of at least one of our species."

Hazel spoke to Sage through the headset. "Sage, they've finally said something that they can all agree on. Use that to your advantage. It may be our only chance in getting everyone on the same page. At least for a while."

Sage whispered, "Point taken." She turned her attention back to the others. "Well it seems we've finally come into agreement. Destroy Meditrina in order to save the species."

Tension flashed in everyone's eyes. Sage wondered if they were going to vanish in the blink of an eye like the other group of vampires. A grin spread across Liberty's face, and she took a step forward. "She does have a point. I'm in." She turned toward Rowan. "It doesn't mean I trust you, though."

Rowan took a step toward Liberty, and for a moment she seemed to growl. "The same goes for me, but since the three of you are willing to put the hatred aside and do this for the greater good, I suppose I could do the same."

"What about you," Sage asked, looking over to the man who had been quiet the whole time. "What are you feeling about this whole thing?" He remained silent. "Well?"

He looked over to Thomas and Liberty and began to sign. Thomas looked over to Rowan and Sage with a smile. "As you can see our friend Simon has a little bit of a problem when it comes to conversation."

"What happened to him?" Rowan asked. She rarely encountered a vampire who was less than perfect.

Liberty chuckled and walked closer, delighted to share this little secret. "He hears perfectly. It's just in his ability to talk where he is lacking." Simon opened his mouth, revealing a black hole where there should have been a tongue.

The girls cringed. Rowan took a step back and turned but kept on looking again like she was driving past a car accident. "That is totally disgusting. I can't believe someone actually did that to you."

"The only thing that made it heal was vampire blood," Thomas added in.

"That is pretty incredible then," Sage added in and looked to Simon. "You were really lucky that a vampire was around then. That would have been a horrible way to die."

Simon nodded in agreement.

"I've seen some nasty things in my life but this one just moved to the top of the list," said Rowan.

Thomas smiled and continued, "The vampire that turned him saw the opportunity and knew what was going on so he decided to help Simon out. By becoming a vampire he was able to take revenge on those that did this to him and help free a bunch of his people. Just a little backstory so you ladies understand where he is coming from." Simon smiled and nodded.

Hazel spoke up again through the headset. "Remind me never to tick that guy off. He is just scary."

"Still, he agrees with everything that we have talked about. Meditrina needs to be killed."

Rowan stared Thomas down. "I don't trust you, but right now this is our only option. You try to come after me at any point, though, and I will chase you down and kill you."

Thomas stepped forward. "Is that a threat?"

"No," Rowan said as her lip twitched, "that's a promise."

Thomas turned to Liberty and Simon. "I think she's starting to like me." All three vampires laughed. Thomas grinned back at Sage and Rowan.

Sage was holding Rowan back, whispering in her ear, "He's not worth it."

Thomas put out his hand toward Sage. "We are all in. For the greater good."

Sage let go and Rowan swung her newly freed fist across Thomas's face, knocking him to the ground. He sat there for a moment, shook his head and wiped the blood off his lip, and said, "You sure you don't want a taste?"

Rowan spat at him, ready to finish him off right then and there. In her mind she shuffled through a dozen different scenarios that ended with Thomas's death. "I don't put any garbage in my system. Why would I start now?"

"I told you she likes me," he said to Liberty and Simon with a cockiness that made Rowan cringe.

"Enough," Sage yelled. "Right now I need you to shake on this so we can get out of here and move on with the plan."

"Are you kidding me?" said Rowan.

"No," Sage said, looking at the both of them. "I need to know that you guys are on the same page for this. One of you may end up having to watch my back."

Rowan and Thomas stared each other down.

They began to reach out to each other when Hazel came over the headset. "We have movement going on upstairs on the catwalk."

Rowan looked at Sage and pulled out her sais. "I told you we couldn't trust these guys." She took off for the catwalk and flew up the ladder with catlike speed. The others quickly followed, Sage informing them that they were being watched.

Sage spoke into the communicator. "Hazel, tell me that you have something for me."

"I am scanning the area and I have nothing."

"Not good enough. Do it again," Sage ordered.

"Do you think it was a rookie mistake?" Rowan whispered. She didn't like saying it but there was a possibility.

Sage shook her head. "No, I heard something in her voice that makes me think this is for real."

"Nothing, Sage. I have scanned the area in all frequencies. Not a single thing came up in infrared, and the same for ultraviolet."

Rowan said, "You're saying this thing just vanished into thin air."

"Y-yes," Hazel said. "To make things worse, this thing wasn't like any of you."

Sage looked at Rowan. "What do you mean?"

"I was checking out the different settings on the scanners and I was using the aura setting when I noticed it. The aura was not like any of the five of you. I'm trying to match it up with research I've done, but I'm coming up blank so far."

"What was its aura like?" Rowan asked, lowering her sais.

"There wasn't one."

Rowan raised her sais again and pointed them at Thomas's throat. "What do you have waiting for us?"

Thomas pushed the weapon away. "Nothing, honest. Now how do I know you didn't bring something to ambush us?"

Rowan growled and lifted the sais back up to his neck. "I would never do something like that. Especially with Sage here. Besides, I think you're lying to us."

"Rowan, he has no reason to lie to us," Sage said. "Do you have any idea what it was, Thomas?"

"No." He looked to the other vampires, who shook their heads.

"Who else knows what is going on? Could it be Meditrina?"

Liberty spoke up. "No one else knows, other than the circle we came with. We took every precaution not to tell anyone that was too close to Meditrina."

Simon began to sign. Thomas said, "Meditrina already has people everywhere. She has made her presence known with the clans. He says if Meditrina is on to us, we may have to move up the attack before she tries to cut it off."

"Agreed," said Sage. She didn't like how this was all playing out but she really didn't like how they had a new uninvited guest. "We will move up the attack as soon as we can form a plan. Still, before we do anything I need you guys to shake hands and agree you will put your differences aside and work together for at least that night."

Simon signed some more, and Thomas chuckled. "He said that if Rowan always moves that quickly in a fight, he'd rather be on her side than the alternative. He's in."

Liberty chuckled and said, "Hopefully they're both that good. I'm in, also."

Thomas looked to Sage and Rowan. "I've been in. So Rowan, now it's you. We've got your back. Do you have ours?"

Rowan looked unsure. She was going to have to help a group of vampires. She would rather they battle it out and kill each other. There would be less work for her.

Sage said, "Rowan, we eliminate her and that's one step closer to saving both of your kinds. No more unnecessary violence. It's a step closer to peace. Also, we might finally get a lead on where my father is hiding out." As Sage finished, Rowan slowly extended her hand toward Thomas.

"This could be the beginning of a beautiful friendship," he said, grasping her hand in his and pumping it up and down.

"Don't count on it. We're not going to be getting together on the holidays anytime soon."

Liberty laughed and said, "Such hostility."

Rowan quickly aimed a sai at Liberty, but she didn't flinch. "They say keep your friends close and your enemies closer. That is all I'm doing." She put her weapons away. A slow clap echoed through the warehouse. Simon, Liberty, and Thomas looked around. Rowan and Sage drew their weapons once more.

Sage got on the communicator and said, "Hazel, I need a report. Someone's in here with us."

"Already on it," said Hazel. "I'm not getting anything. Wait, it's coming from the floor."

"It's coming from the floor. Everyone look down," Sage said, taking her own advice and combing the blackness beneath for the source. "I need more than that, Hazel."

"Okay, whatever it is, it's what was there before. The aura—or lack of—is there again."

A voice echoed through the building, drowning out Hazel's. "Well done, Sage. You managed to unite enemies for a common cause."

"Who are you?" Sage shouted into the darkness.

Before Sage finished talking, someone appeared next to her. He was taller than everyone else. He smiled at Sage, who seemed frozen to her spot, unable to speak.

"Boo!" the man yelled and then started to laugh. Before Rowan could lunge at him, he was gone.

Hazel got on the communicator and said, "Sage, you look like you've just seen a ghost."

"I did."

"Who was it?" said Thomas.

"It was him," Sage said, her voice echoing. She was doing her best to control the anger that was building up inside her. "My father. He was within my reach and I couldn't do a thing."

"Don't worry about it," Rowan said to her reassuringly, trying not to wonder what her father wanted and why he was watching her and not doing a thing. "I know you, and when the time comes and things really matter you will do what you need to do."

Sage looked back at her, frustrated. "There's a part of me that's not so sure about that anymore."

NINE

Late in the evening, Sage's team—with the addition of Thomas, Liberty and Simon—sat in a back room of the darkest, dingiest bar after closing time. Thomas had called in a favor because they needed a place where they could think without being interrupted. Thomas and Sage sat at the bar, out of earshot of the others.

Thomas began to unroll a set of blueprints as he spoke. "Here's the layout of the building."

"How did you get these?" Sage asked, looking over the blueprints.

"That's a good question. A lot of vampires died to make sure I got these."

"Where is Meditrina located?"

Thomas pointed. "She lives here mainly. I've marked where the guards are stationed. She is usually heavily protected." He took a marker and indicated the guards' checkpoints. "There are usually two at her door."

Sage had done similar missions but this was the first time going against a vampire fallen angel. She could run into some curveballs in the process. She needed a good starting point. "How would you recommend we get in?" She didn't know the layout of the building and she wasn't able to do any type of recon. She relied on someone the rest of the team didn't trust. It didn't sit well.

They leaned over the plans and discussed strategies.

"WHY DO THEY call you Liberty? Is that your actual name?" Hazel scrambled for conversation with the vampire next to her. Rowan was tossing darts to relax in an uncomfortable situation.

"It is my actual name. My father was in the military. He ate, slept, and breathed the military life. His children are an extension of his all-American views. It could have been worse."

"How's that?" Hazel asked, smiling.

"I could have been Apple Pie," Liberty said with a chuckle. Hazel joined in. Even Rowan laughed a little.

"What's your story?" Rowan asked Liberty. "How did you...become one of them?"

"I wanted my freedom and to get out from under military rule. I wanted liberty of my own. So I ran away. You know how the story goes. I fell into the wrong crowd and found out I actually liked it. I was offered an opportunity with this guy I'd met at a bar. He was a vampire, although I didn't find that out until later. He told me he could give me the world."

"You went willingly?" Hazel's eyes were wide as she absently ate chips from a bowl on the table.

"Why wouldn't I? You should have seen the guy."

"I-I don't know. I don't think I could ever do that."

"Come on, Hazel. The chance to do whatever you want and never grow old? To sleep all day and party all night?"

"Sounds like you've watched *The Lost Boys* one too many times," Rowan said, throwing in her two cents.

"It is a tempting offer." Hazel looked at Rowan with raised brows.

Liberty continued as though no one had interrupted. "The opportunity to truly feel every emotion, to really be touched." With this last remark, Liberty playfully ran her fingers down Hazel's arm.

"Emotions and I don't get along." Hazel drew her arm away. She was torn. The vampire charm was beginning to pull her in but part of her was turned off by the idea. Rowan knew exactly what Liberty was doing.

"Maybe we should go somewhere else and talk a little bit more," Liberty said with a grin.

Rowan stopped what she was doing and turned toward Liberty, her dark eyes boring into her. "Don't forget to tell her about the killing you have to do to survive. Tell her about the bloodlust."

"That's right," said Hazel, waking up like she came out of a trance. "I don't know if I would be able to do that."

"That's funny coming from someone whose race is just as guilty of murder as mine," Liberty spat at Rowan.

Rowan turned and threw a dart at Liberty, who caught it as easily as catching a lazy butterfly. "Do you want to hear how I became who I am today?" Rowan turned toward Hazel, who was listening intently to every word. "I told you only half the story." She was glad that she wanted to know. Hazel was going to need protecting and that job would fall to her.

"What are you?" Hazel asked, still not sure for herself.

Liberty and Simon both nearly spit out their drinks. "You mean you don't know?" Liberty said.

"No, I don't. So will someone finally tell me?"

Liberty looked over to Rowan with a smirk on her face. "Wow, she really is that green. It's cute. Do you want to tell her or should I?"

Rowan clenched her jaw so hard that Hazel half-expected her to crack some teeth. "Rowan, you don't have to tell me if you don't want to."

"No, it's time. If you are going to be a member of this team, you need to know who I really am. The reason the vampires are giving me such a hard time, the reason this whole deal was so difficult to make, is because I'm their enemy."

"Their enemy?"

"She is what our kind have been at war with for hundreds of years," said Liberty. "Think of what you've seen in the movies. They're not far off."

"You...wait," said Hazel. "Are you a werewolf?"

"Yes, I am a werewolf," Rowan said, her eyes down.

"But you look normal." Hazel's remark caused Liberty and Simon to chuckle.

"Well, normal if you want to—" Liberty was cut off by Rowan's sais pointed once again at her neck.

"That's enough."

"I was only kidding. Can't you even take a joke?"

"When it comes to whom I am, no." Rowan's cold eyes pierced deep into Liberty, finding the little soul she had left. "Don't forget how easy it would be for me to rip your throat out. So Hazel, do you want to know how I came to be?"

Hazel nodded.

"Good." Rowan tilted her head to one side, then the other, as though loosening up for a big fight. "All I told you was that my fiancé was killed by a vampire. The truth is he wasn't killed in the way you would think. He was turned into one of them," she said, to surprised reactions from Liberty and Simon. Rowan ignored them. She was telling this story for Hazel. She needed to know there was a difference between the good and bad in the supernatural world. She also needed to know that some of them, including herself, still had issues to work through. "We got married anyway. I tried to love him, but he changed. He was not the person that I fell in love with. The man I loved was dead."

"So you left him," Hazel said.

"Yes, I left him. He wanted to turn me, and I didn't want too. I had no choice. It was either turn or die."

"You would have made a better vampire than a werewolf if you ask me," Liberty said.

"Let her finish." Sage's voice carried across the tables, and Liberty looked slightly abashed, not having realized that Sage and Thomas were listening to the conversation.

"I was a mess," Rowan continued. "I was young, and had lost the only person that I'd ever loved. My family thought I was crazy." Rowan was pale and shaking. "In some ways I suppose I was crazy. I didn't really care if I lived or died."

"What happened?" Liberty asked, absorbed in the story despite herself.

"I started to drink. It was a way to numb the pain. Back then it was rare to see a woman drinking in a man's environment, so I drank in hiding. One night I heard some people talking about werewolves and some trouble they were having. Like I said earlier, I didn't care if I lived or died at that point. I decided to check it out. It was a chance to distance myself from my husband, and if it didn't work—"

"You were dead," Liberty finished for her.

"Yes, but I was already dead on the inside, so that didn't make a difference. So I began to study what I could about werewolves from books. There was still a problem: I needed to learn how to fight. I spent my life savings learning from these two guys I met at a bar. I think they were fugitives, so it was a win-win situation. They got enough money to disappear, and I picked up what they were teaching faster than expected. They pushed me hard, and I enjoyed it."

"So, the person who had been lost was beginning to find herself once again," Hazel said to her. She wiped her eyes on her sleeves.

"Yes," Rowan said. "Then I heard some stories about this stranger that was in town. It was rumored that any town he visited had bad luck. I decided to check it out, and it was the moment I had been waiting for."

"You found your werewolf," Hazel said.

"I wasn't sure how to approach him. I had a few drinks," Rowan said. "I realize now how stupid that was. If there was ever a time to keep a clear head, that was it."

"Liquid courage. Everyone takes that route at least once in their life."

"Exactly," Rowan said. "I found him, and all I wanted to do was let out all the anger and frustration that I had bottled up inside me for so long. I charged and attacked. He did his best to keep me at bay. He had several opportunities to end it real quick. I should have died. I was ready to die, but the wine kept me from feeling the pain, and he kept me from dying."

"He turned you to save you," Hazel said.

"He saw the pain in my eyes. In a moment of pure anger, I spat the truth out to him. He knew I was ready to die. But he decided on something better for me. He gave me a chance at a new life. He wanted to give me a chance to get revenge on those who had killed my love, and I wanted to take it."

Liberty pushed away from the table. "Wonderful story, but did you ever think that your man wanted to be turned in the first place?"

Rowan threw all her weight forward as she punched Liberty in the mouth, knocking her back and causing her to bare her fangs.

Sage rose from her seat and moved toward the others. She grabbed Rowan and Liberty by the shirts and pulled them close. "We can continue the story some other time. Right now we need everyone to play nice for the next twenty-four hours. After that, I don't care. Rip each other's heads off. But as long as you are working with me, save it for the bad guys." She tossed the two of them back into their chairs. "Now, are we cool?" The two looked at each other in venomous silence. "Well, are we?"

"Yes," Rowan was the first to say.

"Fine," Liberty said.

"Good. Now why don't you guys join us so we can go over the plan."

LATER THAT NIGHT, the girls were back in their room getting ready for the oncoming fight. Rowan was in her bedroom meditating, and Sage was sitting on a chair near one of the windows, reading.

Sage put her book down when she saw Hazel approaching. "Something on your mind, Hazel?"

"Yes, something is bugging me about Rowan's story. How did she find you and become part of your team?"

"The werewolf couldn't give her what she wanted," Sage said.

"What was that?"

"It could be one of several things: love, family, friendship. He gave her a chance to get revenge, but then there was nothing left for her. She was back where she'd begun. That's where I found her and helped her."

"You helped her find the vampires who had turned her husband?"

"No," Sage said. "That was done a long time before, with the help of the man who made her into a werewolf."

"How did you help her, then?"

"I gave her freedom," Sage said with a smile. "I gave her a chance to be who she wanted and not be known as Lucius's creation."

"He's the one that made her? What happened to him?"

"He's still out there somewhere, for all we know." Sage opened her book again. "The same goes for her husband."

"He's still alive? Why hasn't she…I mean, that's got to be tough."

"Yeah. She'll tell you that story when she's ready. She likes you. It's been a long time since I've heard that story."

"Wow," Hazel said, flattered by what she just heard.

"Oh, and Hazel," Sage began. "Don't worry; it will all come to you in time."

"What do you mean?" Hazel sat down at Sage's feet.

"How you get ready for it all," Sage said. "Each of us gets ready for battle in our own personal way. Rowan meditates and prays to her gods."

"What do you do?"

Sage smiled and once again closed her book. "I read," she said, holding up the book, which was covered in old paper bags. There was handwriting all over it.

"What are you reading?"

"The book that reminds me why I am doing the things that I have done for so long. It focuses me back to the core." Sage handed the book to Hazel.

"What language is this?"

"Go ahead and take the cover off. I can put it back on." Hazel pulled the cover off, revealing a white, faded cross on the original cover.

"The Bible," she said. "You read the Bible before you go to battle. Why? I've never read it so I'm just trying to make some sense out of something I have seen in the last twenty-four hours."

"It reminds me about what is going on around us. That there is an evil out there, and it needs to be stopped," Sage said. "Look." She took the book back from Hazel and flipped through the pages until she found what she was looking for. "It says, 'Woe to those who call evil good, and good evil. Who put darkness for light and light for darkness. Who put bitter for sweet and sweet for bitter. Woe to those who are wise in their own eyes and clever in their own sight.'"

"That's great and all that," Hazel said, "but what about me? What about someone who isn't at that point like you? How do I find that?"

"I am willing to talk whenever you are ready to," Sage said softly. "I can help you find your way."

"I don't know. I just need some time to think." She got up. "Maybe I just need to go for a walk."

Sage knew what she was going through. A long time ago, Sage had been in the same position and the person that helped her knew not to force the issue as well. "No problem. Whenever you want to talk about it, I'm always here for you."

"Thanks," Hazel said and headed for the door. "I'll be back in a little while."

"Don't be too long. Business starts in a little while."

AFTER WALKING BACK into town Hazel found a little spot away from most of the crowds. She people-watched while her mind went in a hundred different directions. *What in the world did I get myself in to*, she thought. In the last ten days her eyes had been opened to a world that she had never known was there. It was a world that held so much darkness, with only a few signs of light—Sage's team. *All this to find the one that made me lose my sister.*

A passerby gave her a funny look, and she wondered who they were. No one was who they seemed anymore, and part of Hazel was okay with that. "If it means getting my sister back, I will do whatever it takes," she said out loud. "Even if it means playing baseball with the devil." She smiled and thought, *who knows, I might actually figure out who I am supposed to be.* She figured she should head back before the others wondered where she was. She was walking toward the hotel when Rowan materialized out of the darkness.

"There you are," Rowan said, scanning the area for any trouble.

"What are you doing? Did you come out looking for me?"

Rowan cheeks lit up. "All the new people that join the team go through what you are going through. I wanted...I just..."

"You wanted to come and check on me," Hazel said with a smile.

"Well, yes."

"You aren't as tough as you come across. You like me, whether you'll admit it or not."

"Never said anything like that. Don't let it go to your head. Let's get going." Rowan turned to go without waiting to see if Hazel would follow.

Hazel caught up with her. "You like me, and you want to be friends." Hazel barely refrained from poking Rowan in the side.

"Just don't expect us to be painting each other's nails and doing our hair anytime soon," Rowan said back with a reluctant grin.

"We can work on that," Hazel said. "You aren't as tough as you come across."

"You say that around anyone else, and I will show you how tough I can be." Rowan's grin faded before Hazel could be sure it had even been there at all.

"All right, G.I. Jane. I was joking, let's go."

TEN

Sage's team sat in their surveillance vehicle on a random corner in the city. Rowan and Hazel were leaning over the monitors, which displayed pictures of the Asylum: the club and vampire fortress that Meditrina had taken over and made her own.

Sage stood in the front of the vehicle, talking to her team. Thomas, Liberty, and Simon were toward the back, half-listening.

"This is the Asylum, otherwise known as Meditrina's home base. It used to be a warehouse and was converted into a nightclub. On the upper levels is the sanctuary for her and her minions. The lower levels is the club, and it's basically an all-night buffet for her and the family."

"Absolutely disgusting," Rowan said, feeling her skin crawl.

"How is it different than what you do?" Thomas asked.

Rowan stood up. "At least I don't make it a carnival game. I give what I hunt a fair chance."

Thomas grinned. "Really? Listen here, sweetheart, your kind is more like us then you think. The sooner you realize that, the better off you will be."

"What's that supposed to mean?" Rowan stepped in their direction, ready to challenge any of them.

"What? You mean that thought never crossed your mind?"

"What are you talking about?" Rowan asked.

"What would happen if the vampires and werewolves joined forces? Think of the hell we could raise together." He was pushing her buttons, egging her on.

Rowan snarled and stared Thomas down. Her blood was boiling as it raced through her veins. She looked to Sage. "Can I kill him now? I can do it real quick; it would make our lives that much easier, and I can finally get rid of this headache."

"Enough." Sage stepped between the two of them. "We need to finish this mission. After that, I am so over the two of you bickering that I don't care what the hell you do to one another."

"I'm all for that," Rowan said with a smile.

"Same here." Thomas stepped back.

"I agree," Hazel said, eyes still on the monitors. "The whole thing is disgusting, but the setup is brilliant. They never have to leave if they don't want to. How will we know if we truly have her?"

"I'm part of the few that has actually seen her," Thomas said. "And she has a way of making herself known."

"Isn't that ironic?" Rowan turned to Sage. "Still think we can trust him?"

Sage answered, "That's why he stays with me."

"What, and you get to kill the bad guy again? You get to have all the fun."

Sage rolled her eyes. "If he stayed with you then one of you wouldn't make it through the mission." She turned to the rest of the group. "Look, we need to stay focused. The plan is simple. This isn't going to be prime hours, so hopefully we won't have a lot of humans on the scene, and we might take the vampires by surprise."

Liberty looked at her. "Might take them by surprise? Do you plan on walking right in the front door?"

Sage smiled, looking to Rowan, Liberty, and Simon. "That's what you guys are going to do, and I want you to make as much noise as possible. You will be the distraction that Thomas and I need to get in."

Liberty grinned. "I don't think noise will be a problem."

"This sounds pretty dangerous," said Hazel. For the first time in a while, the group laughed together. "I'm serious. Has anyone considered that I am the only human here?"

"But that's the fun of it," said Rowan, still grinning.

"Don't worry, I think we know very well that you are a human," said Liberty. Thomas laughed at her remark, and Simon smiled.

"Hazel," Sage said, "you don't need to worry. For this mission I need you back in the truck watching for anything odd. Especially if my father pays a visit."

"Good," Hazel said with a sigh of relief. "I don't think I'm ready for field work yet."

Rowan looked at her and spoke. "After this is done I will start training you. I'll turn you into a warrior in no time." The vampires laughed and Rowan stared them down. "The next time you see her, she will be able to take all of you on at once and win."

"We'll have to test that theory," Thomas said.

"Well, being in the truck will give me another chance to research Meditrina some more."

Thomas turned to Hazel. "Why do you still want to do that?"

"I would feel more comfortable if you and the rest of the team knew who you're going against. I want to find any weaknesses, to give you guys an advantage."

Sage nodded. "That works for me." She looked at Thomas. "Why do you care what anyone on my team does?"

"I was just curious," Thomas said. "I already told you, I know what she looks like, so Hazel doesn't need to do any of that work. She should be keeping an eye on you guys." He walked over to Sage and grabbed her hand. "I wouldn't want anything to happen to you."

Sage pulled her hand away. "Whatever, Thomas. Just focus on your part of the plan."

Rowan stepped between them. "You can never be too careful. Once they know we're in there, they're going to be coming at us with everything they have."

"These guys aren't playing with cap guns either," said Thomas. "The Asylum comes well equipped to defend."

"Why aren't you dead, then?" Hazel asked Thomas. "If you're so outspoken against her cause, shouldn't she have killed you already?" The question made everyone pause and stare at Hazel.

Thomas walked over to Hazel until he stood only a few inches away. "I left before she took control. My former employer was one of the clan heads that Meditrina took out to get control. I was his bodyguard."

"I wouldn't put that one on your resume," Hazel muttered, looking down. Something bothered her about every move Thomas made.

"It was a small miscalculation. I made a mistake I don't plan on making again." Thomas turned away and paced the small area.

"I don't buy it," Rowan said.

"Are you going to let her talk to me like that?" he asked Sage. "I came to you for help. Why would I lie to you?"

Rowan smiled. "I'm just saying, Hazel's the psychic around here. She might have a point." She moved closer to Thomas in the cramped space. "Is she right? You would tell us, wouldn't you? I mean we're all friends here." Rowan showed the tips of her wolf fangs.

"You put her up to this, didn't you?" he fired back at Rowan, his back to the wall of the truck. "This was your way to get back at me. Well, I'm not buying into this crap."

Sage stepped between Rowan and Thomas. "This stops now. There will be no more talking about anyone's past."

Rowan laughed and walked toward Hazel. "I'm impressed, kid. You're showing some spunk." She turned to Sage and said, "You know she is a psychic. She may have something here."

"Psychic?" Thomas repeated. "Why is she on this team? She can't even fight. Next she's going to be babbling on about blue monkeys. This is all a bunch of crap. I'm putting my life on the line here, and now I'm the one getting crucified." He looked to Sage. "Are we going to do this or not?" Without waiting for a reply, Thomas got out of the truck and stormed away.

Sage looked to the rest of her team. "Yes, we are going to do this. We will talk more about this later. Right now I need you both to do your jobs." Sage left to catch up with Thomas, who has already turning the corner.

Liberty and Simon looked at each other, and Simon shrugged his shoulders. Liberty nodded. "You're right." She grabbed her bag that had been sitting by the side of the truck and started to follow Thomas and Sage. "Come on, Rowan. Let's go make some noise."

Rowan looked at the bag. "What do you have in there?" Suspicion laced her tone. Regardless of the joint cause, she couldn't shake the distrust she had of everyone but Sage. These creatures had been her sworn enemies for so long.

"I wanted to make a loud impact," Liberty said and laughed. She showed Rowan the inside of the bag, and Rowan's eyes opened wider. "I always have that kind of backup in my bag. They would never miss a couple of them. You never know when you'll need to wake the neighbors."

"You may not be as bad as I thought you were," Rowan said. Liberty smirked and walked off.

ELEVEN

I'm telling you, something doesn't smell right with Thomas," Hazel said to Rowan over the communicator.

"You know I'll have your back on this, no matter what." Rowan kept her voice low but still caught Liberty's eye.

"What are you talking about now?" she asked.

"Hazel's trying to decide if she should watch the new episode of the *Walking Dead*, or not."

Liberty flipped her off, and Rowan blew her a kiss. Rowan picked up her pace and whispered, "Just do what you have to do to keep Sage safe. Now we stop talking about this and focus on the task at hand."

"Read you loud and clear," Hazel said as she saluted the image on the computer screen.

"Good, now tell me what we're looking at up ahead. I don't want any surprises."

"All right," she said, tapping out a rhythm on her keyboard. "There are hardly any vampires down in the club. They're probably all getting ready for tonight. Uh-oh, it looks like there could be some humans in the club."

"That could be a problem," Rowan said then addressed the rest of the group. "Hazel said there are some humans left in the club."

Liberty looked over. "They might just have to be causalities of the battle."

"Not if I can help it," said Rowan.

"Why do you give a damn about them? If the shoe was on the other foot do you think they would care if you lived or died? They would hunt you down like the dog you are."

"Maybe I'm taking a page out of Sage's book. Maybe if I am an example of good to the world, some people might follow my lead."

"Interesting, a werewolf with a heart. Wait until some of the other vampires hear about this," Liberty said, laughing. "Especially when they find out that it is the legendary Rowan."

Rowan made a beeline straight for Liberty, once again letting her emotions get the better of her. "I should just kill you right now." She tackled Liberty to the ground, throwing punches wherever she could find flesh. Simon grabbed the back of Rowan's coat and used all of his strength to pull her up while Hazel yelled at her through the communicator.

"Stop it. Stop it now, Rowan. Get ahold of yourself," Hazel yelled.

Rowan stood up, wiping her lip on her sleeve. "What's he saying," Rowan said, gesturing to Simon, who was signing furiously.

Grudgingly, Liberty answered. "He says we're acting like children. Oh, that's good. He's calling you out on what you said earlier about leading through example. He wants to know what kind of example you are being now." Rowan growled at Liberty, who put her hands up in defense and pointed at Simon.

"Look, Rowan," Hazel said, "I know you're tough, but there is no reason that you can't have a heart either."

"I don't need to be hearing this from you, too."

"I know you're a warrior, and some of the best warriors knew the difference between right and wrong and weren't afraid to stand by their morals. You just happen to be someone like that," Hazel told her. "Now you know what you need to do."

Rowan took a deep breath, and tried to hide her grimace. "Look," Rowan said to Liberty, "I...I didn't...."

Liberty, who was wiping the dirt off her face, looked up at Rowan. "I know. Me too." Liberty looked abashed for a moment but quickly recovered. "Now that we have all this touchy feely garbage out of the way, we need to figure out how we're going to get inside."

"Rowan, you are not going to like this," said Hazel, "but I have an idea that should get you in without a problem."

"I don't like the sound of this." Rowan shook her head. She knew it would work but didn't like what she had to do. Rowan looked to Simon and Liberty and told them the idea that Hazel had.

"I, on the other hand, like the idea already," Liberty said with a laugh.

A SHORT AMOUNT of time later. Liberty and Simon led a disgruntled Rowan in zip ties being used as cuffs toward the club.

"Hazel," Rowan growled, "remind me to hurt you when we get done with this."

"Why? This is a good plan. The vampires would smell you five feet from the building," Hazel said, showing off some of the knowledge she'd acquired over the last couple of weeks.

Liberty looked over to Rowan and down at the cuffs on Rowan's wrists one more time. She wanted to make sure they were on tight enough, but also wanted to let Rowan know how she felt about an issue. "You've got a good one there with Hazel. Keep a close eye on her and teach her well, otherwise I will come looking for you."

"Don't worry," Rowan said, "I'm not planning on seeing you guys after we're done here." Simon tapped both of the women on their shoulders to signal that it was time to play their parts. "Here we go," Rowan said.

ON THE OTHER side of the club—along the back alley—Sage and Thomas were doing their best to go unnoticed by the people walking through the back doors.

"It looks like we may have gotten here a little later than we should have," Sage said to Thomas, trying to do her best to blend in with the crowds.

"Probably because this town hasn't seen something like this club before. It's drawing attention from everywhere," Thomas said. "It has always been that Hollywood and places like that always made evil the prettier one. Meditrina just made it more accessible. Now people are going to be able to immerse themselves in it."

"Got any ideas on what to do if we're seen?" Sage asked.

Thomas grabbed her and pulled her in close, catching Sage off guard. She felt his breath on her cheek. He pushed her hair off her neck, and Sage's heart raced. Thomas leaned in and whispered, "I can always play like I am getting ready to bite you. Heck, you could let me. That would be convincing."

Sage pulled herself together. "Or we could just hide." She pushed Thomas away. His advances had been cute at first. Now she was beginning to find them annoying, "That would be just as easy and I wouldn't have to remind you that I like the person that I become involved with to be living, not dead."

"Sweetheart..." Thomas laughed as he let her go. "I was only kidding. Tonight is all business for me. I will save the pleasure for later, you can join me if you want."

"Don't count on it," Sage said, just as they came across a side entrance.

"It looks like we are finally in," Thomas said, then moved aside and opened the door with a flourish. "Ladies first."

TWELVE

There was a bouncer at the door, about six-foot-five. He made some NFL linebackers look small. The remnants of his hair formed a mohawk, and the tattoos on the side of his head were there to intimidate. Liberty was prepared to walk right past the man, certain that as long as she showed no fear, he wouldn't give them any trouble. The big man shoved his well-muscled arm in front of them.

"Why do I smell a werewolf?" the bouncer asked.

Liberty laughed. "Well, sir." She emphasized the title, grinning even wider. "Maybe it's because we have one right here." She gestured toward Rowan.

"Excuse me?" the bouncer said.

Liberty pulled Rowan forward and presented her to the man. Rowan did her best to avoid making eye contact, which was not a comfortable position for her.

"This isn't just any werewolf. This is Rowan. The one that runs with Sage McKenzie. We found her snooping around, and my partner and I managed to catch her. We decided that we should bring her to Meditrina. We thought we might get some kind of reward."

"Hmm," he said, staring down at Rowan. "Let me call upstairs. Come on in. You'll fit right in with all the festivities that are going on tonight. The mistress will be happy to know that we now have a werewolf to add to the mix. Maybe we can have someone fight her for fun?"

"Maybe we could," Liberty said, glancing at Rowan. "But I will say one thing. This werewolf knows how to pack a punch. I had to wrestle with her for a bit, but I eventually broke her spirit." The bouncer laughed as he walked over and got another vampire to cover the door so he could make the call.

Liberty led the others in with her. They had walked into a lounge area. A few people were sitting at the bar. The three of them went as far from the bar as possible and tried to melt into the shadows.

"We don't have much time. Scary guy is making the call, and if we don't move soon we will get caught for sure." Liberty cut the cuffs off Rowan and handed her the sais that she'd been storing in her bag.

"Thanks," Rowan said and took a deep breath. She felt complete once again.

The main room boasted all the vices that a person could think of. There were dancers on pedestals wearing so little that you didn't need any imagination to get the rest of the picture. Those that weren't dancing were flirting with the small crowd gathered in the room. The alcohol was flowing, and there were a few gambling tables as well.

"All right, we need to split up to cause more chaos," said Rowan. "When I give the signal, we start making some noise." They all split up to cover more ground. In a few minutes, the bouncer came back looking for them.

He saw Rowan sitting on one of the couches with her hands behind her back as though she was still tied up. "Great, where did they go?" he said, looking around. He turned to look at the crowd. He put a hand to his headset to call the rest of security when Rowan stood up.

"I wouldn't do that if I were you," she said, pointing her sais at the back of his neck. He turned around faster than Rowan would have thought possible and put his hands around her neck. Rowan tried to use the sais to counter the attack, but he lifted her into the air before she had the chance. Just as her eyes were nearly level with his, she raised her knee and kicked him in the groin. The bouncer dropped Rowan, and she rolled out of the way, jumping up with her weapons raised. She scanned the room to see how many humans were around before anything else happened. She saw a few at the bar, talking. She ran to the bar where Simon and Liberty were also waiting and yelled, "Now!"

Two vampires popped up from the shadows and ran toward Simon and Liberty. Liberty opened her bag and grabbed one of the low-end training grenades she had rattling around. They were more show than go, but she was more interested in causing trouble than making any real impact. *Explosions and alcohol makes the start of a real good party*, she thought.

The first explosion went off as Rowan finally got to the group of people that were sitting at the bar. Rowan yelled, "I need you guys to take one last drink and get out of here. That explosion was the first of many, and it's not part of an act."

"No." One guy looked at Rowan. He oozed cheap cologne and stood too close to Rowan while he was speaking. "We paid a big cover charge to get in here. They said we weren't going to know what was real and what was part of the show. Well, we want to see a good show."

"Look," Rowan said, "I was trying to be nice about this, but you're asking for the hard way." She pulled out her sais and pointed them at the group. "You need to get out of here now, or I will run this into places that will make you hurt for weeks." The group moved slowly, still unsure whether this was part of the show or not. "At least go out onto the patio," Rowan said shoving as many of them as she could outside.

THE HALLS WERE surprisingly quiet for the time of night.

"Thomas," Sage whispered as she hid behind some plants. The halls in the upstairs of the building had a high-end feel to it. "Something's not right here. Why haven't we run into anyone?"

"Relax, Sage," Thomas said, joining her behind the plant. "The Meditrinala is tonight, and anyone that is in the building, especially those that are vampires, are getting ready for the big show tonight."

"That's why we need to find her quickly," Sage said, beginning to move down the hall again.

Thomas reached out and took her arm. "I know," he said, "that's why I'm supposed to lead, right?"

"Right, sorry. This place is giving me the creeps," she said, taking in some of the vampire art that lined the halls. The paintings showed the bloodlust in a very "Hollywood" fashion. The faint sound of an explosion reached their ears, and Sage pressed herself up against the wall for a moment, breathing heavily.

"It looks like Liberty dropped her welcome card," Thomas said with a chuckle. "She sure likes to make an entrance."

"Grenades," Sage said with surprise. "What, does she think we are going to war?"

"Would you expect something less from a woman named Liberty, sweetheart? Like the saying goes, 'Give me liberty or give me death.'" Thomas peeked around the corner to see if it was clear. "Besides, that is exactly what might be coming. These vampires are looking for power. They aren't stopping now that she is in control of all the clans. Meditrina wants the town."

THE EXPLOSION BROUGHT in more security, which caused Rowan, Liberty, and Simon to change their plans a bit. The small crowd in the lounge began to scatter in blind panic, but in the main room it was business as usual. The crowd in that room was too caught up in their surroundings to even notice what was going on.

"Do you have any other brilliant ideas?" Rowan said, looking at Liberty. Simon pointed up to the catwalk that was around two sides of the main area of the club. There was movement up there.

"It seems like we were on the guest list after all," Liberty added. They counted six members of the security team up on the catwalk.

"I hate to say it," Rowan said as she focused in on them, "but at least three of them are carrying weapons. That's not acceptable for me."

"Unless those are silver bullets in those guns," Liberty spoke as they were looking for a better place to plan their next move, "they won't harm any of us."

"I know that, and I bet they do too," Rowan said. "But that means if they use them it's going to be for one of two things: slowing us down, or taking out unnecessary targets."

"What's your plan?" Liberty asked.

"I don't like it, but I think the best option we have right now is to split up," Rowan said reluctantly. Sage had instilled the "strength in numbers" attitude in Rowan early on, but she could see no other option.

Simon shook his head, and Liberty said, "I'm with him on this one."

"It's the only way we can divert the attention of those vampires that have the weapons. If they have to look for three of us individually, they have to split up, too."

"Fine," Liberty said, noticing that some of the security guards were heading their way.

"All right, good luck guys," Rowan said. She stopped for a moment. "Man, I really am starting to get soft." She shook her head.

"You see, you are beginning to like us after all," Liberty said, before running off in the opposite direction to Simon.

The security split up, just as Rowan had hoped they would, but some of them were still coming her way

"Hey, buddy, you looking for me?" She pulled out her sais and went into attack mode. The vampire smiled and charged. Rowan used some of her pent-up anger on the vampire. She made quick work of him with a few quick swipes of her sais.

Rowan laughed as she returned them back to her holster like a gunslinger. "That felt good," she said to no one in particular. She looked up to the catwalk and decided that it was time to head up there.

Hazel chirped on the communicator, "Rowan, I see you. I hope you're not thinking about going up there. That isn't a good idea. You'll be trapped."

"Sorry, but that is a chance I will have to take," Rowan said and looked back up to the catwalk.

THIRTEEN

Liberty made her way to a part of the building where the chaos hadn't hit yet. She did her best to calm down and try to blend in with the other vampires. The room she had come to looked like a harem, and the women vampires were playing the part of seducing the men that entered the area. She looked around and saw an elaborate and expensive-looking water fountain. She reached into her bag and scrambled for another grenade. Her hand wrapped around the cool metal, and she pulled it out and took a step forward.

"I wouldn't do that if I were you." The voice was deep, and almost seemed to echo around her. One of the members of the security team had found her already. She scanned the area but found another security guard waiting at the nearest exit.

Liberty knew she could hold her own in a fight with two vampires. She wasn't anything like Rowan, but she wasn't useless either. She reached into her jacket and pulled out a large hunting knife with a serrated edge on one side. In one swift move, she thrust it into the security guard's shoulder. The vampire pulled back as the knife pierced his flesh. Those nearby watched in fascination, some of them smiling at what they thought was an elaborate part of the show.

"Wonderful special effects," someone said. "They had to have spent some good money on that."

"You shouldn't have done that," the security guard yelled. Liberty pulled the knife back out and was knocked off her feet by two other security guards. The knife and her bag went flying in different directions. Liberty continued to throw as many punches at the two vampires as she could, but they took her down without much difficulty.

"Is this any way to be treating a lady?" she shouted at them, still trying to draw attention to herself. They got her under control and stood her up. The vampire that had been stabbed found the knife and picked it up. He walked over to Liberty and grinned. He wiped the blade across her jacket.

"I told you that you shouldn't have done that," he said, frowning. Suddenly he altered his grip on the knife until the tip was pointed at Liberty's shoulder. Taking a good look at her, he said, "Besides, someone as young as you shouldn't be playing with knives." He plunged the knife as deep as he could into Liberty's shoulder. She let out a yell and some of the crowd that was watching the action cringed away from her piercing cry.

"Damn, that hurt," Liberty said, once she'd recovered slightly. "What's your name?"

"They call me Snake," he said.

"Really? Snake, is that a nickname that you gave yourself because you were lacking in..." She let her gaze drop for a moment. "Other areas?" Two of the security guards holding her stifled laughter.

"My actual name is Francis," he leaned in and said a little quieter.

"Wow," she said, trying one last time to draw some attention, "I actually got caught by a guy named Francis. On second thought, you should stick with Snake."

"Why did you want to know that?"

"I make it a point to know the names of all the vampires I kill," she said then spit in his face.

Francis wiped the spit off his cheek and told the two other security guards to lock her downstairs. "That's one down and two more to go," he said, looking at his shoulder that was already healing up.

HAZEL HAD MANAGED to hack into the security cameras and watched helplessly as her team took a beating. *This isn't good,* she thought. *Something isn't right. I need to let Rowan know what just happened.* Hazel got on the communicator. "Rowan, we have a problem."

"What's that Hazel," she said, sounding slightly out of breath from climbing the ladder to get to the catwalk.

"Liberty has been captured," Hazel said.

"Damnit," Rowan said. She pulled herself onto the catwalk and punched a wall. "I thought she would last a little longer than that. Any word on Simon yet?"

"Nope," Hazel scanned all the camera feeds she was able to get. "Maybe we can go with the 'no news is good news' thing?"

"Let's hope so," Rowan said. "Just try to find him, and while you're at it see if you can find out where they took Liberty. Got to do a rescue now as well as take down the bad guy and kill a bunch of vampires. But you know what?"

"What?" Hazel asked.

"I like those odds."

"I understand. Oh, and Rowan?"

"Yes?"

"Be careful," Hazel said. "I think they may have been expecting us."

"If that's the case then we are all in trouble," Rowan said. "Have you managed to contact Sage?"

"That's what is so strange. It's like someone is trying to jam her communicator on purpose."

"Then we'd better be ready for anything. Keep me posted."

Hazel went back to work on the computer, trying to find out any-thing she could on who Thomas really was and anything else she could find out on Meditrina. "Come on Hazel," she said, fear taking a firmer hold on her. "You are better than this. Don't let the fear get you. You know what you are doing. Now just find something that is going to help these guys beat her." She went back to searching on the network that Sage had created, hoping she wouldn't be too late.

SIMON SENSED THAT the plan was going bad. All he had to do was turn around, walk out of the building, and just keep on going. He could leave this town, especially since things were starting to get out of hand here. There were other places he could go. He was old and had made many connections through his lifetime. Then he thought about it more. If Meditrina's plan really began to take effect, things could get bad. He was certain it would lead to them being hunt-ed once again. Although they were hunted now, it was only by a very small percentage. If things got ugly, then anyone and everyone would be hunting them. It would be as common as hunting—deer season, duck season, and now vampire season. Plus, if he went on the run, he would be alone. He would have friends here and there, but if Medit-rina's army kept on gaining momentum, he would be hunted by his "friends" as well.

Besides, what about Liberty? She had been traveling with him for a while now, and the two of them had become awfully close. He couldn't leave her behind. She was younger than he was, and she would be able to survive, but he was really beginning to enjoy her company. He knew what he had to do.

He couldn't help but wonder if the others had made it inside. The downstairs had a simple design. There was no elaborate artwork or deco-ration in the hallway. He began to wonder how big this place really was and how long the building had existed. Once he had an idea about its origins, he could begin to figure out if all the hallways on that level were worth exploring. He continued to make his way down the hall, trying his best to not look out of place.

Simon had a hunch that the coven would be in the basement. It was out of the way and secluded enough that any noise they made wouldn't disturb the guests in the club. He began to check some of the rooms as he passed. It was interesting that the vampires around here had no real idea what was going on upstairs. That at least gave Simon a bit of relief. He reached a door that was crimson and had a brass knocker hanging from the center.

Simon opened the door and found several female vampires in various stages of undress. The ones that were dressed looked as if they were in some type of costume. He had stumbled into the dressing room for the female vampires. There was a stairway in the corner of the room, which must have led to the stage in the main room.

Simon tried to back out without being noticed, but it was too late.

"I see someone thinks he can get a free look," one of the women said, grabbing him and dragging him back inside the room.

Simon attempted—in vain—to pull away from the woman, feeling the blood rush to his face.

"It seems the cat's got his tongue," another woman spoke up. The group circled him like vultures, giggling. "Then again, what should we expect when a man walks in and sees all of this around him," she continued, motioning to the women. She was a tall blonde, strapping up her top in preparation to go on stage. Simon put up his hand and motioned for the ladies to stop. To his surprise, they obeyed. He opened his mouth and showed them why he wasn't able to speak. The ladies flocked closer to him.

"You put new meaning to the strong and silent type," the first vampire said. She began to run her hands down his chest, feeling some of his scars from when he was a slave. The other female vampire that had spoken to him walked over and ran her hands down both of his arms.

"I see what you mean," she said with a smile. "He is definitely strong and not like any of the other vampires around here."

Simon was losing focus. He needed to get back out to the hallway. He wasn't used to the attention that he was getting from these women, and he was beginning to like it. He was used to being treated like a freak.

"Perhaps you would like to stay for a little while and keep us company," she said to Simon with a gleam in her eye.

Simon's head began to spin, and his palms began to sweat. He had no idea how to respond to this attention. One of the vampires began to kiss his neck, then another one did the same.

"OH NO," HAZEL said, wondering what was going on behind the closed doors that Simon had just disappeared behind. "This isn't good. I need to figure out what is going on."

She was almost positive that this whole escapade had been a setup. She was just trying to figure out who the mastermind had been. Liberty was out of the picture because of what had happened to her. Besides, Hazel didn't think Liberty was as hungry for power as the others. There was actually a small part of Hazel that liked Liberty. Not that she'd be telling Rowan that anytime soon. Then there was Simon. She wasn't convinced that he was innocent in all this, just because he was off her radar at the moment, and that worried her. He wasn't an easy person to figure out, especially as a man of few words.

Plenty of questions were raised when it came to Thomas. Hazel wanted to know why he had shown up out of nowhere with this whole problem going on in the first place. Everything seemed too convenient. On the other hand, Hazel couldn't come up with a reason why Thomas would do this to Sage. She couldn't see what his motivation for such an elaborate scheme would be.

Hazel began to wonder why she hadn't heard anything from Rowan in a while. Bad thoughts began to run through her head. *What would happen if they were all captured,* she wondered. She would have to leave the truck and go out there on her own, despite not knowing a thing about fighting. "I need to stay focused."

Hazel started to make a checklist of things she should do next. It was the only thing she could do to get herself refocused and back on track. She quickly ran through the list, knowing that time was short. She needed to reach Rowan and tell her about her suspicions. She had to get through to Sage and find out what was jamming her signal to warn her. Quite unexpectedly, Hazel stumbled across something on the computer. "Shut the f…front door," Hazel said into the empty truck.

She quickly got on the communicator. "Rowan, are you out there?" Hazel said. "Talk to me. This is urgent stuff I've got here."

"I would love to chat right now," Rowan said, breathing heavily, "but I'm busy, and I don't need you to start shooting me the latest possibilities for a nickname."

"Forget about that. You need to know this. *Now.* You have to get out of there. I found the security footage of the murder of Thomas's old clan leader. He helped her do it. Thomas helped Meditrina set the whole thing up. He works for Meditrina."

"THOMAS!" ROWAN SAID. She swung her sais over her head and brought them down toward the vampires she was fighting. "I knew it. Sage should have listened to m—" She was cut off when one of the vampires blocking her exit nicked her arm. "Damn, now I'm bleeding, too." Rowan looked for an alternative exit, but there were two more vampires heading up the only other way out. She launched into her attack, her mind racing. "Hazel, I'm in trouble here. I don't know how much time I have to talk to you."

"Don't say that. I don't have a clue what to do. I have no idea how I'm going to get you guys out of there."

Rowan said, "Don't worry about us. We have been in worse situations than this." This was at least half true. They had been in worse situations, but at least in those instances they'd had a plan to escape. This time Rowan didn't have the slightest idea how she was going to get out. "If I get captured, I need you to do whatever you can to get to Sage and tell her what you found. Then you need to get the hell out of here."

"Stop talking like that," Hazel said, sensing worry in Rowan's voice for the first time since she'd known her.

"Drive away from here," Rowan continued as though she hadn't heard Hazel. The vampires drew ever closer. "If they knew we were coming, then they know that you are out there. They just haven't found you yet. Just get out of here, *now*," Rowan screamed the last word and looked around. She was cornered. She looked down and had an idea. If she was going to get captured, then she would do it on her terms. She looked over the edge of the catwalk again, judging the distance. It wasn't that far down. Especially if she could make the jump toward the stage.

"I NEED TO get somewhere else and drive away. Just for now." Hazel babbled to herself as she struggled to move to the front of the truck. In her haste, she dropped the communicator in the back of the truck. Once in the driver's seat, she started the ignition, and the motor roared to life. Hazel hit the gas before the truck was in gear; when the engine screamed at her, she stopped and took a breath. She looked toward the Asylum and noticed a few vampires pointing at the truck. Before she was able to do anything, they jumped into a nearby car and began to head in her direction. "Dang it, dang it, dang it," Hazel said as her blood pressure began to rise. She threw the truck into gear, and she was off down the road, heading directly toward the vampires in front of her. Hazel noticed, almost absently, that she was hyperventilating. Her sister's face swam through her head, that day she had disappeared. The same blind panic was gripping her.

They had hidden in the little space in their closet as the killer had broken into their house and slaughtered their parents, leaving them all alone. Tears blurred her vision as she stepped on the gas a little harder. She wasn't going to let fear control her in this situation. She was going to do what she needed to do so she could survive. She continued on the path toward the two vampires, who had realized what was going on, and had accelerated toward her, too. So now it was a game of chicken. Hazel's fear began to turn into anger as she continued to drive straight toward them.

"Come on, you stupid vampires," she shouted as she drove. "Just get out of the way," she pleaded with them. No one was backing down. At the last possible second, Hazel swerved just enough to miss them head on. Hazel kept on driving, needing to get away. She needed to get somewhere that she could think and begin to form some sort of plan.

ROWAN LOOKED AT the vampires that were starting to come at her from each side. She smiled and waved. "See you later, boys. I can't let you get me that easily." With that, she slid her sais into their sheaths on her legs and leaped over the railing. She grasped a hanging light and held on.

She got some momentum, swinging back and forth, and jumped toward the stage. She crashed heavily onto the DJ. Rowan staggered up as the crowd looked around to see why the music had stopped. For a moment, Rowan wondered if the trance they were in had been broken. Even the vampires that were dancing on the stage stopped what they were doing to watch.

She looked back up at the catwalk, and the vampires she'd been fighting seemed frozen as they watched her. They knew that someone had to be on the crazy side to attempt that kind of jump. She waved, took a few steps, and then cried out as she felt a pain radiating up her whole body, beginning at her ankle. She was done running. She fell to the ground, and some other members of the vampire security team rushed the stage and surrounded her.

"I said you weren't going to get me that easily. I never said you weren't going to get me at all." She held up her hands in surrender.

The vampire called Francis stepped onto the stage and said, "I am sorry for the interruption, ladies and gentlemen, but that was just a little situation from a guest that wasn't on the VIP list. In fact, that was a were-wolf." The crowd booed, thinking it was all part of the show. Some other members of the crew got on stage and helped the DJ, and soon the crowd was back to having a good time.

"Well, well, well. If it isn't the legendary Rowan. The muscle of Sage's army. It's funny, but it seems like we managed to catch all those that were going to try and crash tonight's celebration."

"You haven't caught Sage," Rowan said.

"That's where you are wrong," Francis replied.

"She will figure out that Thomas was all part of the plan, and then she will destroy everyone." Rowan tried to sound fierce, but she was feeling the pain in her ankle even more.

"She doesn't even realize what she is walking into," Francis said with a devilish grin. "You are the guests of honor. This party was a way to take out the few who actually stood a chance against Meditrina. She has a very special offer for Sage McKenzie. She wants to offer her something that you can't give her."

"What's that?" Rowan said, doing her best to hold on as the pain in her ankle worsened.

"Meditrina is going to offer Sage her father," Francis said with a smile.

"Her father?" Rowan didn't like the sound of that. They were playing right into Sage's one weakness: the quest for revenge. The worst part about it was they had all walked into it oblivious to what was really going on. "Why would she do something like that?"

"Meditrina said she knows how to get to him, and she will give her the army she needs to destroy him."

"Now we really are screwed," Rowan said, his words fading and growing distant. And then everything went black.

FOURTEEN

Hazel sat alone on the hood of the truck, crying. She could see the Asylum in the distance. Its lights were blazing, drawing everyone in to their impending doom. She was confused and angry with herself. Once again she had run from trouble. It wasn't that she had wanted to, it was more that she didn't know how to deal with the situation. She had done the same thing when she'd left her sister at an orphanage in the condition that she was in. She hadn't known how to fix the problems, so she'd run away. This was still a whole new world for her, and she had no idea where she fit into it. She had no answers and knew that it was only going to be a matter of time before the vampires caught up with her. She felt desperate. Hazel didn't know where to turn so she went the only way that seemed like it made sense.

"God, I have no idea what I'm doing right now, and I don't know if I'm doing this right, but I need some help. My friends and I were taking on some bad guys and the plan went wrong, really wrong. They're all in serious trouble, and I am the only one that has any chance of saving them. I need some answers, direction, anything. I am tired of running. Please help me." She let everything go, and she began to cry in earnest. It was a release, something that she needed to feel, as well as something that she hadn't felt in a long time. After everything that had happened, she stopped allowing herself to feel. Tonight, she did. A peace came over her. She felt like everything was going to be okay.

In the distance, a horn blasted. It was unlike any sound she'd heard before. There was silence for a moment, and then she heard what she was certain must be a motorcycle. She tensed, preparing to run if it was a vampire. The rider got closer. Hazel felt herself getting stronger. The motorcycle stopped about two feet from her. The man driving was bigger than the average human being, and from what she saw, he had armor on his chest. It was barely visible underneath the modern clothes he wore. His dark hair flowed in the wind and was as long as his duster. His bright blue eyes had the strength of armies in them.

"Are you ready to go save your friends?" he said.

Hazel felt safer with every word he spoke. "Who are you?" she asked, jumping down from the hood of the truck.

"I'm Gabriel," he said as he sat tall. "You asked for help. So I was sent to help you."

At that moment realization struck Hazel, and she half-curtsied, half-bowed, unable to make up her mind about what she should do. She wanted to show this man all the respect he deserved.

"Don't bother with any of that," he said as he got off his bike. He walked like a warrior. "From what I can tell, we really don't have a lot of time. I want you to know that it's all going to be okay. My friends—" Gabriel laughed, and it was like he was laughing at a joke that only he knew the punch line for. "—My friends and I are going to help you all out of this mess. You can watch everything from the back of the truck. We will do all the dirty work."

Hazel didn't know what to say. She was relieved that the cavalry had shown up to help, but she was also mad that she was getting told to wait in the truck once again. "What if I want to help you? These are my friends, and I can't stay back and do nothing. Not again."

"You did do something," Gabriel said. "You asked for help, and you got it. You did something that you never thought you were going to do.

You called out to the one that could help you, and you turned it all over to Him. Even if you don't believe that you have it, you showed faith."

Hazel realized he was right. She was still mad she couldn't do more, but deep down she knew that she'd done more than enough. "I still want to go after these guys. They messed with my friends," she said.

Gabriel looked at her, and Hazel felt that his heart ached for what she was feeling, "When the time comes, you will know when it is your turn to fight. This isn't what you went through with your sister. This is a bigger battle, and it is going to be the first of many to come. You have a place in this. But you have some work to do. You keep doing that work, and you will be ready to fight in no time."

"I understand." She didn't like it but knew he was right. Her day would come when she would fight along with the others.

"Good," Gabriel told her. He knew Hazel lacked confidence, and he was going to be the one to help her gain it back. "Why don't you get back in the truck and lead the charge?"

"Gabriel, sir, how does one do that? I have never lead a charge before."

"Just Gabriel is fine. All you have to do is drive. We will follow you."

"Okay. You keep talking your friends. Where are they?"

Gabriel smiled. "Don't worry," he said. "You will see them soon enough."

Somehow, she knew that she would, and with that she turned and got in the truck and started it up. She felt a tingle of excitement run down her spine. Help was on the way and everything would be all right.

She put the truck into drive, and she heard Gabriel's horn blast once again.

THOMAS LED SAGE down some more hallways. "Are you sure you know where you're going?" she asked.

"Of course I do," he said, trying to show he was in complete control of the situation and had a plan the whole time. "I have been here many times when the previous owner had it. Meditrina changed some things up, but there are only so many things you can do in a month. You know, I think there's a place we need to check out that is right down this way."

"The hallways are really quiet around here," Sage said as she continued to look around.

"Everyone is chasing the other three around, no doubt," Thomas said with a smile. "All right, here we go. I think I found what I was looking for."

AS HAZEL WAS driving she began to wonder what she could do to un-jam the signal so she could speak to Sage. Suddenly she had an idea and quickly pulled the truck over.

"What's the matter?" Gabriel asked, pulling up beside her.

Hazel opened up the back door of the truck and saw her communicator sitting on the floor. She picked it up and tried to call anyone that would hear her. "Rowan," she yelled, "are you there? It's me, Hazel." There was no answer. She tried again, trying not to act nervous as Gabriel watched. "Rowan?" She looked over at Gabriel, panic creeping back through her body.

"Don't worry. They might have captured her with the others. What we need to do right now is get there so we can rescue them."

"That's not the reason I stopped," she said, and went to the computer. "I think I have a way to give Sage a warning."

"Go for it," he said, climbing into the truck with her.

"Why can't you just use a little of your angel magic and help me out on this one?" Hazel asked, remembering who she was talking to.

Chuckling, he said, "Hazel, it doesn't work that way. We are not magical genies that can grant your wish. You still have to do some of the work."

"Heck, it was worth a shot." Hazel continued tweaking the computer's communicator program.

"Hopefully this will work. I just hope we won't be too late."

ROWAN CRIED OUT in pain as she did what she could to help speed up the healing process of her ankle.

"Quiet down there," a familiar and annoying voice yelled from one of the other rooms.

"Liberty, is that you?" Rowan asked, already knowing the answer.

"How is it that the big bad warrior managed to get herself caught, too?"

"I rolled my ankle jumping from the catwalk."

"No way," Liberty shouted back, and Rowan heard true admiration in her voice. "You are one sick woman. You really jumped from the catwalk?"

"Yeah. It wasn't my intention to get caught by these guys."

"Yet here you are."

"Didn't say it was one of the smartest things I've ever done. But it didn't kill me." Rowan shook her head again as she looked down to her ankle that was quickly healing.

"Is Simon here?" Rowan asked, wondering if everyone had been caught. There were four rhythmic bangs against one of the walls.

Liberty sat back in her cell and nodded, though no one could see her. "That sounds like him. How is it that we all managed to get caught?"

"According to what Hazel was figuring out in the truck, Thomas set us up."

"He was working for Meditrina the whole time?" Liberty asked. Simon banged on the wall. "I agree, that bastard. So that leaves us with Hazel? It's all up to her?"

"Yes, it's up to Hazel. She's the only one that can help us now." The three sat in their separate cells, wondering the same thing: what the chances were that they would all get out of this alive.

THOMAS LED SAGE into a room with a lot of art in it. It was all Gothic style. There were dark scenes that usually depicted some innocent person getting attacked by some vampire. Sage felt a chill run through her body as she saw everything that was on display. She continued to walk forward as she felt herself being drawn to what was in the room. She saw an iron maiden sitting in the middle of the room, as well as other medieval torture devices.

"You guys have some really sick taste," she said, looking closer at the iron maiden. "Seriously, where do you even—" Sage turned to speak to Thomas, but he was gone. "Thomas?" she called, looking around for him. "This isn't funny. You can stop joking around." She looked around some more but there was no sign of him, just morbid darkness. She headed toward the door when Thomas walked back inside.

"There you are," he said. "I thought you were still behind me, then I turned and you weren't there."

Sage took a breath. Something didn't feel right. "Don't you ever do that to me again."

"You didn't think I was going to leave you here on purpose?"

"Can we just get back to doing what we came here to do?"

"Sure," he said, heading out the door that they'd come in.

"Sage…" Hazel's voice crackled over the communicator. There was a lot of static. Sage moved around, trying to find a better signal but found none.

"What's going on?" Sage asked. They had never had problems with the communicators before, and Hazel's voice did nothing to calm Sage's worries. "Hazel, is everything okay?"

"Everyone has been captured," Hazel said, speaking clearly and slowly.

"Did you say everyone's been captured?" Sage felt herself get short of breath. A chill ran up her spine. Thomas looked over, trying to hear what was going on.

"I managed to get away. I got real lucky."

"Good," Sage said. "Where are you?"

The static grew heavier. "Don't worry about me. I need to…" Hazel's voice faded.

"Say that again, Hazel," Sage said. "The static is terrible in here."

"I said…" The static grew worse. Sage looked around for better reception. She glanced at Thomas, and he shook his head.

Silence filled the room and then suddenly Hazel's voice came back on the communicator. "There's something I need to tell you."

"What is it?" Sage asked. The lights in the room flickered off and then on again. Her heartbeat quickened; something definitely wasn't right. She began to move around the room frantically, trying to find someplace where she felt more comfortable. Someplace where she could see what was going on.

"This whole thing is…" Hazel's voice managed to cut back in once again. The lights went out once more, and Sage felt something strike the back of her head. It was too late. She fell to the ground.

FIFTEEN

"Wake up." Sage felt ice cold water and a few ice cubes hit her face. She felt like a sledgehammer was using her head for a cymbal except she couldn't stay in beat. Metal wire bit into both wrists, keeping her strapped to a chair. Every time she moved the wire tore into her flesh. She opened her eyes and didn't recognize the room. *Thomas.* She wondered if they'd gotten him, too. She continued scanning the room and noticed Thomas bound to a chair about two feet to her left. He looked as woozy as she felt. Sage tried to remember what Hazel had been trying to tell her. She hoped the others weren't in a similar situation, however, things weren't looking good.

The room appeared to be a large meeting hall with a huge glass atrium that shone with stars. The sun had been setting when they started this mission. With the night sky outside, she couldn't tell how much time had passed.

She took in her surroundings, trying to use the room to her advantage. At the closer end of the room, an attractive woman sitting in a chair stared at her. She wore a Belle Époque jacket, almost like a tuxedo top, but with a skirt on the bottom that flared to a handkerchief hem.

Fingerless gloves and studded leg warmers completed the look. Sage continued to look around the room and saw that there were twenty to thirty others sitting along the sides of the hall. She figured they were vampires who were part of Meditrina's new group, waiting to watch the festivities for the night.

Sage noticed that Thomas was moving. She tried to get his attention, and he finally looked over to her. She whispered, "I guess that's her?"

Turning, he looked around the room and saw the woman. "Yes," he said. Sage got a good look at the damage the vampires did to him.

"Man, you really know how to make friends around here. Was this part of your plan to get us inside?"

"I wasn't planning on it going this way. But heck we're in, aren't we?" Thomas laughed, but then stopped and clutched his side.

"Silence," Meditrina said, her eyes chilling everyone in the room that still had a heart. "So, this is the great Sage McKenzie? I have heard much about you. So many annoying things. You have been nothing but trouble to some friends of mine." Meditrina got up and walked toward her two prisoners. Once she reached Sage, she extended a hand toward her face and ran it down her cheek. Sage felt the chill of death in her fingertips. "You know, there is still one thing that surprises me. As a half-breed, I expected you to be…"

"Harder to catch?" Sage jumped in, still trying to figure out what had gone wrong with the plan. Suddenly she remembered the tracking device Hazel had convinced Sage to put in her left boot. Immediately she began trying to activate it, reminding herself to thank Hazel when this was all over.

"Yes," Meditrina said, pulling back to look at Sage. "I certainly expected you to be harder to catch, but I also expected you to be much… taller." That got a laugh from the crowd.

"Well, if you don't mind me saying, as a fallen angel, I expected you to be…"

"Yes?" Meditrina said, her face clearly challenging Sage.

"Prettier," Sage said with a smirk. She knew that would sting Meditrina. Any of the beauty she'd had as an angel would be overshadowed by the vampire blood.

Meditrina slapped Sage across the face with the back of her hand, her rings biting into Sage's flesh. The slap echoed through the room.

Meditrina glared at Sage with eyes of the devil. "Don't play those head games with me, child. I am the one in charge here. You are done talking. You will not speak unless I tell you to. Do you understand?" Sage slowly turned to face Meditrina, eyes burning as she spat blood at her.

Meditrina laughed as the blood landed on her arm. She raised it up and licked it off with a smile. "You taste sweet," she said, licking her lips. Sage tried to fight her way out of the chair again, still getting nowhere. Meditrina laughed as Sage struggled. Then, in one swift motion, she knocked the chair on its side. Sage crashed to the floor and smacked her head on the concrete as Meditrina turned away.

"I guess that wasn't the best thing to say to her, but her communication skills are to die for," Sage said, doing her best to shake the cobwebs out of her head and trying to figure out why she was on the floor.

Thomas grinned. "That's one of the things I love about you, Sage. You always have a way with words."

Meditrina began to pace in front of the waiting vampires, as though she were about to address them all. Instead, and much to Sage's surprise, she turned back to them and addressed Thomas instead. "I thought you said you would be able to convince her to join up with us," Meditrina said, turning back and facing Thomas.

Sage's heart froze. Now things were starting to make some sense.

Thomas shook his head.

"You let her get to you already? The charade was meant to last a little bit longer."

He slipped out of the wire ropes easily and walked over to kneel in front of Meditrina. "I am sorry, my queen. I did the best I could." He pointed at Sage, who was still on the ground. "She's just thick and doesn't understand what we have to offer her."

Sage began to laugh. She finally understood what Hazel had been trying to tell her.

"What's so funny?" Meditrina asked.

"That you sent forever frat boy to whisk me off my feet and show me that your way is the better way to go. Do you know who I am?" Sage said.

Meditrina glanced down at Thomas. "Ladies and gentlemen, it seems that our honored guest tonight wants to know if we know who she is. I think that I should show her."

"First I want to hear what Thomas's part was in all of this," Sage said as Meditrina motioned to two nearby vampires who lifted up her chair, righting it and making sure she was still bound to it.

"That's a good idea. Why don't we let him explain why I didn't have him kill you on the spot." Meditrina looked down at Thomas. "My dear, the floor is yours." Meditrina went back to her chair and sat down comfortably, waiting for Thomas.

Thomas's injuries were quickly fading as he walked to the center of the floor and looked around at the crowd. He then directed his full attention toward Sage.

"For those who don't know, I was once employed by one of the former clan leaders. I was the head of their security detail when Meditrina approached me. She told me her plan to unite the clans under one rule." Thomas swung his hand around to encompass the whole crowd in the room. "The vampire race is to rise again and take its rightful place on this earth. Heaven belongs to God, and this world belongs to the Devil. The time has come for us to serve the master the way we were meant to serve him and bring him the earth on a silver platter."

Thomas looked to Sage and stepped toward her. "Do you want to know why I played this game with you? It's simple. When I told you that I cared, I did. My feelings for you were legitimate. Eventually I came up with this whole plan, which had a good chance to work. I wanted to show Meditrina that you would be a good addition for us, and you were the one that was able to unify races. You would be the one able to end the war between vampires and werewolves. If you joined us, we would be just that much stronger. Then we could end this war we have with God and the angels. You would be able to help bring all those that God rejected and unite them. We would win and then we would have this planet and do what we want to do with it."

"Lofty goals for someone that still has a hard time trying to land dates," Sage said, flustering Thomas with her comment.

"The whole thing came down to the fact that I could offer you the world. Better yet, *we* could offer you the world." Thomas motioned to the crowd, and then grabbed Sage by the shoulders. "Still, you had to be so thick-headed about it. You wouldn't even give me a chance to explain it to you." He stopped and let go. Sage heard the frustration in Thomas's voice and knew he was starting to lose patience with her. "I tried to show you how loyal your friends were. I was pushing Rowan's buttons and playing her like a flute. She was a loose cannon and couldn't be trusted. Hazel is weak and innocent, and when it came down to it, she still wouldn't be able to save you. And that in the end, you are still alone. You and I are more alike than you think. The only way to truly exist is to side with us." The crowd of vampires applauded at the end of his speech.

Sage looked at him. For a moment, she was actually impressed. She hadn't realized how well Thomas would thrive in situations like this. Still, she looked at him and thought that, for every positive thing, there were twenty bad ones. She wasn't going to fall for his magical voo-doo. "I should have known all along that you were nothing different than the rest of these bloodsuckers. I should have let Rowan kill you when she asked."

Thomas laughed. "I would have loved the opportunity to finish off that annoying dog."

"Don't worry, when she comes this time, I will give her the chance to take you down." Sage grinned.

"I am looking forward to it. For as long as I have known you, I have waited for that chance."

Meditrina stepped forward. "Such problems are between the two of you. Quit acting like you're married. Let me offer you something, Sage, which will sweeten the deal for you."

"Nothing you say will make me want to side with you." She considered spitting again but thought better. "My blood is too good for you."

"What if I told you that I could give you the one thing that you want the most?" Meditrina took a step closer to Sage. She circled her, gently running her fingers over her arm and leaned in. "I could give you your father," she whispered in her ear.

"H-how would you do that? You're telling me you would give him up to me?"

"I have ways," Meditrina said. "I have a lot more friends than you think. We walked out of that tomb together with those other fallen angels. The group of us are all connected. We have all waited for the opportunity when some moron would open the gate. Humans. Their curiosity always gets the best of them. Besides, do you really think I wouldn't be able to find him? I would even give you your own demon army to hunt him down and do what you want with him. I'll even let you choose the demons. How's that for raising the stakes? All the world in the palm of your hand. You wouldn't have to search anymore. You could get your revenge, and then enjoy the rest of your life." Meditrina chuckled. She laid all her cards on the table and got Sage right where it hurt the most. "Just a little something to think about."

"I-I have to think. I need to think about this." The offer caught her completely off guard. The chance to finally get her revenge for her mother's death. A chance to finally stop fighting.

"I'm glad you are beginning to see things my way," Meditrina said. What was one fallen angel eliminated when it came to world domination? If everything went according to plan, there would be plenty of the earth for all of them to be able to rule. "We could be a very powerful team."

"You're right, we could be," Sage said. Things would be so easy. Meditrina clapped her hands, and the whole room began to empty until only she and Sage remained. Sage looked at her and had a hard time trying to figure out if she was beautiful or not. The more she looked at her, the more Sage saw the vampire that she had become and not the fallen angel that had once been a creature of God.

"Remember what I am offering you. You will finally get a chance to get the revenge that you have wanted all these years. He wouldn't be able to hide from you anymore."

Sage knew she was right as the sounds of those words pierced deep into her heart. "I understand what you are saying."

"I will be back in ten minutes," Meditrina said. Her smile showed her confidence. "Then I expect your decision." She turned and walked out. Her heels clicked against the marble and echoed throughout the room, reminding Sage how alone she really was. The door closed, and Sage let out a deep sigh. "I'm in trouble," Sage said, knowing there was a part of her considering this offer.

HAZEL WAS SITTING in the truck doing her best to keep her cool. Sage was missing. Rowan, Liberty, and Simon had been captured, and she was sitting there trying to figure out a plan with the Archangel Gabriel. *So this is what a regular work day is like. No one back home would ever believe that I would be doing something like this*, she thought. This made her giggle before she sobered at the thought of Sage trapped in the Asylum.

"Sage..." Hazel spoke into the communicator. She banged her head against the keyboard when there was no response. She looked toward Gabriel, trying not to lose her mind. "I lost her again. This time, however, it wasn't me. Something happened to her."

"Did you try to pick her up on the tracking device you put in her boot?" he asked.

"I didn't think about that." Her nerves were getting the best of her.

"Hazel, I need you to take a deep breath, and remember this is Sage. Nothing bad is going to happen to her. She is better than you think she is, and I have seen her get out of worse jams. Then I need you to activate the tracking device and find her. If she is in trouble I need to know. You can do this."

Hazel took a deep breath and knew that Gabriel was right. This was Sage McKenzie. She was a hunter and one tough woman. "Okay, I will let you know as soon as I have something."

"Good." Gabriel placed his hand on her shoulder. "If this works it will make what we need to do a whole lot easier, and there will be fewer battles that have to happen."

Hazel began to punch information into the computer. "You're telling me. I sure hope this works."

ROWAN PACED, HER ankle already beginning to feel normal again. There were a bunch of unanswered questions lingering around, and all of them had something to do with Thomas. She wanted to know why he would do this, and what Meditrina wanted with Sage.

Then she began to worry about Hazel. She was still so new to this game. Rowan wouldn't have blamed Hazel if she'd just gotten on the next bus and hightailed it out of town as fast as she could. Not everyone was made for this kind of life, especially someone that was still human. She realized she actually liked Hazel and didn't want anything to happen to her.

Rowan knew she had to escape and the sooner the better. She did the only thing she could: she became a werewolf. Since she was older this was a bit easier than it would have been for a younger werewolf, and she did have the practice. They heard her scream in the cell next to her, and it sent chills down their spines. Transformations were never an easy task, and Rowan knew that once she let out that scream her time was limited. She had to work quickly, and she hoped when the guards came to the door it was a small enough number for her to handle.

Within minutes the transformation was complete, and Rowan was in her werewolf form. She began to use her strength to open the door, but wasn't having much luck. She began clawing at the walls, trying to make her way into the other cell, so they could all work together. But she wasn't getting any results other than wearing herself out.

Rowan took a moment to catch her breath, and a voice came over a hidden speaker in the cell. "Stupid girl," the voice said with a laugh. She knew right away it was one of the guards that had put her in the cell in the first place. "How long until you realize that we built these cells to hold people like you? Don't you remember we are supposed to be at war with your kind? Why would we make these cells werewolf friendly?"

Rowan growled. *They should come in here, and I'll remind them exactly what happens when they cage a werewolf.*

As if reading her mind, the voice said, "Just change yourself back. We aren't going to come in there and deal with you until we need to."

Rowan growled again as she thought, *Don't worry I'll be ready for you when the time comes.* There was only one problem: when you force the transformation, it's hard to know just how long you'll be able to maintain it. It would ultimately come down to a matter of wills. Who was going to budge first, them or her? Rowan was going to do her best to make sure it wasn't her.

SAGE WAS STILL deep in thought, trying to figure out what to do. To give up everything that she knew and thought was her life for the opportunity to go after the one thing that had been alluding her for years. She couldn't forget that she would also have the army that she needed to destroy him at her disposal. It was a tempting offer. *Besides, I'm not getting any younger*, she thought. She was tired of running into one dead end after another.

On the other hand, there were those that she helped and the evil that she had stopped from spreading. What about those people? Those women whose crosses she had carried so they could get their lives back in order. *But who am I to do that?* Sage thought. She was not God. He was the only one that could do that, although she had given those women their freedom back.

She began to realize that there was part of her that wanted to be done with all of this, and that thought scared her. Thomas entered the room, and Sage immediately felt bile rise in her throat.

"Now you know the truth," he said as he walked closer to her, almost stalking her. She was now seeing his true colors and what he really was and now she began to understand what everyone else saw in him from the beginning. She couldn't figure out what it was that made her see him different from everyone else.

"Why?" Sage asked, trying to make sense of the whole thing. "Why play such an elaborate game if you just wanted me?"

Thomas pulled up a chair and sat about a foot away from her. He studied her face for a moment. "Sage, sweetheart, it was all about power. I was a nobody until Meditrina came along. I was someone's head of security, and that was it." He stood up. "Now, I'm going to be the general in the vampire revolution. When the first phase of Meditrina's plan is complete, we will own this town and no one will be able to stop us." He sunk into his chair, eyes glazed as he thought about the future. "Hell, if all goes well, maybe I could run this town while she continues on with the plan."

"When will it be enough?" Sage asked. She felt the rage course through her veins. Sage was one to never get played. This time she had, and that was something that she was never going to forget. "Will you ever be satisfied?"

"I would have been satisfied if you'd taken one of my offers when I first met you," Thomas spoke sincerely and scooted his chair closer, reaching to brush some hair out of Sage's face. Suddenly he was like a different person. The lust for power was gone from his eyes, and he looked softer, kinder. "That would have been all I needed."

"What if I had taken the offer? What would you have done when Meditrina showed up at your door?" Sage probed, searching for his weak spot. Something that was buried under all that dirt and grime that made Thomas who he was.

"It's tough to say. It would have made things that much harder to decide. Do you still think I'm the forever frat boy?"

"Yes. The only difference is you're a smarter frat boy now. The one that is always the pompous jerk."

"Even when things look bad you still manage to joke around," Thomas said.

"What do you mean by that?"

"Everyone is captured. It's only a matter of time before we capture Hazel. That girl really knows how to be a thorn in someone's side. She'll be fun to catch. She doesn't know what we do to humans. It will be fun to hear her scream. After that there will be no one to stop us from having the biggest bloodbath sacrifice the world has ever seen."

"Get to the point, Thomas." Sage paled but attempted to keep her voice steady.

"I am telling you that if you don't side with us, there is no way you will walk out of here alive."

"Then I guess things are pretty bad."

"Stop it, Sage," Thomas said, tossing the chair aside. "Don't you see? Meditrina is going to come back here in another five minutes, and she is going to ask what your decision is. If you decide not to join, then someone will kill you. After that they will kill your little team. No one will make it."

"I understand. There's just one question I have for you. When the time comes and you are about to die, which one of us do you want to do it? Rowan or me?"

He let out a shriek and stormed out of the room, leaving Sage alone once more.

"Come on, Hazel," she whispered into the emptiness. "I hope you have a miracle up your sleeve, because things are not looking good."

✠

GABRIEL AND HAZEL waited down the road a ways from the club. Hazel looked at him, took a deep breath, and clenched her hands together to still them from shaking. "What's the plan?"

Gabriel thought for a second and took a deep breath. His armor shone underneath the duster he was wearing. A battle was coming, but he needed to keep as many people as he could out of it. "How good are you at hacking?"

"I know a thing or two."

"Can you get into their system and trip the alarms without getting any of the authorities involved? I want to get all the people out of there but don't want the police or fire department showing up."

"That makes sense," Hazel said. She began to work on the computer, trying to get into the club's system.

"Make it happen. We don't have much time."

"Why's that?" Hazel clicked away at the keyboard.

"The mass sacrifice begins at midnight," Gabriel told her. Hazel picked up speed. "And we're sitting ducks. A vampire patrol could stumble upon us at any moment."

THE DOORS TO the hall were suddenly thrown open, and Meditrina's minions entered and sat down. Thomas entered soon after and avoided eye contact with Sage. He was followed by Meditrina. She wore a beaded, black satin halter-top dress with a slit up to her thigh in the front. She was overdressed compared to the drab vampires skulking about. She smiled at Sage as she walked to the chair in the front of the room.

"Tonight everyone has gathered to hear from the great Sage McKenzie. We wait with baited breath to see if she is going to take the very lucrative offer that we made to her. If she sides with us, she will be given everything she needs to finally do the one thing that she has been waiting to do for years." Meditrina stood and began to pace around the room. "She will be able to kill her father."

The crowd cheered as Sage watched. She realized, more and more, just how disturbed these vampires were.

"Tonight, with the help of Thomas and my elaborate plan, we brought her here." Meditrina walked over to Sage, who was sitting perfectly still. "What's your answer, Sage McKenzie? Are you with us, or are you against us?"

Sage lifted her eyes to Meditrina and smiled. "First, I would like to thank everyone for your gracious offer. It is very tempting. And then to have someone like Thomas present it to me in such a way..." she paused, letting her words sink in. The crowd applauded and Thomas smiled. "...I realized very quickly it was a bunch of garbage."

The crowd gasped. Thomas shook his head in disbelief. "You really think I would buy into the whole idea of becoming the superior race? Meditrina, you had a better chance to get me than sending him." She jerked her head in Thomas's direction. "When he told me that you have all my friends... Well, sister, you just made things a whole lot harder for yourself."

Meditrina laughed. "You think your idle threats scare me? Do you realize who you are talking to? Perhaps I should kill you right now."

"But you won't," Sage said, hoping she was right.

"You're right. I have a better plan for you." Meditrina looked over to Thomas. "We have guests here tonight. Our friends wanted a show, and I think we should give them one. Release her."

Thomas stared, gaping at Meditrina. "My mistress, what are you talking about?"

"You have disappointed me, Thomas. I will grant you a second chance. You are lucky enough to have the opportunity to make it up to me," she said, flashing her fangs in his direction in what was evidently supposed to pass for a smile.

"How?"

"Kill her," Meditrina said with a gleam in her eyes.

"You want me to kill her?" he asked, unconsciously untying Sage's bonds and reaching for his short axes.

"No, you stupid fool." Meditrina sat back and got comfortable. "I want this fight to be fair. Like I said, you disappointed me. Whoever wins will be forgiven, and the loser, well, you know what happens to them."

"I can't fight her."

"Are you saying that you can't fight her because you care for her, or are you just trying to question my power?" Meditrina asked, her voice terrifyingly soft. She reached down to the side of her chair and pulled out Sage's sword, studying it. "Impressive weapon," she said. "In the short time I have been back on earth I have heard several stories about Dragon Claw. You have killed many with it."

Sage stood in front of Meditrina, watching her, but also keeping a close eye on Thomas. "Yes, I have killed many. None that didn't deserve it, though," Sage confirmed.

"Are you up for killing one more?" Meditrina asked. "Doesn't Thomas deserve to die? He did betray your trust."

"If I have to," Sage answered. Meditrina tossed her sword in the air before she finished speaking. Thomas reached across and knocked the sword down with one of his axes.

"It seems like he wants to fight after all," Meditrina said and clapped her hands together in manic applause.

"I didn't know we were fighting dirty," Sage said to Thomas.

"It's survival, sweetheart, no hard feelings when I kill you." Thomas took a high swing, and then another low one with the axes. He grazed Sage on the leg, and she fell to the ground, rolling quickly onto her stomach. "It looks like this may be a quick fight after all." Thomas kicked Sage's sword away and then swung the axes down. Sage just managed to roll out of reach. She opened up her angel wings, gaining a look of surprise from Meditrina. Sage swung the weapons toward Thomas, slashing his left arm.

"She appears to have plenty of fight left in her, Thomas," Meditrina said with a laugh, delighted that the show was going well. As she was watching the action, Francis appeared at her side, and whispered into her ear.

"What do you mean someone activated the alarm system and people are running out of the club? This isn't how it is supposed to happen," Meditrina said. She grabbed a glass vase and threw it at Sage. It shattered as it hit her. "This is all your fault."

"How could I have done it?" she said, her breath coming in quick gasps as she darted one way, and then another to avoid Thomas's wild swings. "You have my entire team, and Hazel...Hazel is..."

"That one..." Meditrina looked at Thomas. "The one that was standing up to you. How is she doing this? You assured me she was weak, yet here she is, the last one of Sage's team to be caught." She looked back to Francis and said, "Get your men ready. There is a new attack coming."

HAZEL AND GABRIEL sat in the truck watching the various video feeds from the club. They scanned the screens, attempting to catch sight of Rowan or Liberty. They also looked at the crowds of humans, attempting to see if Hazel's plan was working. They needed the people to leave the building quickly so they could continue with the plan.

They waited. Music could be heard from the club. Two minutes seemed like an hour, and Hazel was getting antsy. "When are they going to start coming out? The alarms should have gone off by now." Then, as though summoned by Hazel's question, the alarm sounded above the music. An announcement from the DJ followed, telling the people they needed to head toward the nearest exit.

Finally, people began to trickle out. The trickle soon became a flood as the humans pushed past each other, eager to escape. It was chaos, and the spell they had been put under was broken. Tonight was the grand reopening of the Asylum; the people escaping collided with the line of people waiting to get in. They shouted a warning to leave as they exited the club.

"You made sure that none of the emergency departments are getting this?" he asked.

"Yep," she answered, showing Gabriel the work. "By routing everything this way, it goes straight to the club and bypasses the emergency response system."

"You make it sound like you've done this before," Gabriel said, squeezing her shoulder and grinning.

"Well…" Hazel wondered how much she should tell him. Then she remembered who she was talking to. "You probably know this already, but after my parents were murdered and I left my sister at the orphanage, I needed to be able to survive. I did that by learning a new trade. I learned about computers."

"Interesting. Do you regret doing any of it?"

Hazel pondered a moment. "Actually, I don't. I did what I had to do to survive. I never hurt anyone. I also didn't take anything from those that were bad off. I just wouldn't have been able to sleep at night if I had done something like that. It was my version of school, and I graduated at the top of my class."

"I don't think I have ever met anyone like you." Gabriel looked intently at her.

Hazel smiled. "Thanks, I think. I've never met anyone like you, either."

"I think your plan worked."

"Yeah!" She punctuated the word with a clap.

"Nicely done. Now get ready for something really cool."

"I can't wait to see what you have planned," she said excitedly.

Gabriel stood up and grabbed a lead pipe that was lying by the side of the road. He dragged it across the ground, drawing a line in the sand. He walked back over to his bike and pulled out his horn and blared it. The sound of motorcycles responded. It was a loud roar that shook the ground beneath them.

Gabriel set his horn down and began to speak as he walked. "My brothers, the time has come." The motorcycles were getting louder. Hazel looked around, attempting to see where they were coming from.

"We have waited for the right moment for years. Now I call to you, my angelic brothers." Gabriel raised his voice to be heard over the motorcycles. "Come now if you are ready to fight. Come now if you want to destroy evil with me. Let's ride tonight as warriors. Let's ride tonight as angels of death to those that oppose the most high." He reached behind him and pulled out his scythe. He raised his arm over his head, the blade extended, and a line of angels appeared, all on motorcycles. They were dressed exactly as Gabriel, their armor partially hidden by modern clothing, with faces so beautiful they could have been chiseled in stone.

Hazel quivered, her knees weak from the sudden appearance of dozens of angels. "David Copperfield has nothing on you," she shouted, still trying to catch her breath.

Gabriel turned and smiled. "I told you I had some friends with me." He turned back to the angels, looking regal. This was his rightful place, a warrior general of legions of angels. "My friends, say hello to Hazel."

The angels turned as one to wave and shouted, "Hello."

"Hello, boys. Now go and get my friends back," she shouted, wishing she had a flag to wave to make this sentiment more powerful

"Okay," Gabriel shouted to his troops, "let's ride." With a thunderous roar, the motorcycles began to move.

ONCE THE LAST two groups of people had disappeared down the block, Francis looked at his men. There were ten of them altogether, and they were all big enough to participate in an MMA event.

"Hazel?" Francis shouted as they walked back through the main area of the club. "Are you in here? Come out, come out wherever you are." There was no answer, and Francis realized his men were beginning to stare, so he turned to address them. "I want you to spread out and find her. Bring her to me alive. I want to be the one that serves her head to Meditrina on a silver platter."

"Yes, sir," several of the vampires shouted, and they began to spread out. They had all heard the stories of how Meditrina acted when things didn't go her way. Some of the stories claimed that Meditrina had lost her mind. One of the security guards looked over to Francis and said," I never want to be on Meditrina's bad side."

Francis nodded. "Keep your eyes open. I don't think this is the only thing that's going to happen tonight." Too many things were happening already. It felt like the calm before a storm. He reached into his pocket and pulled out a large, jagged hunting knife. Just as the rest of the security men were pulling out their own weapons, the sound of a horn echoed through the streets, followed by the roaring of motorcycles.

"Is that thunder?" one of the vampires asked, looking over at Francis with uncertainty. "I thought tonight was supposed to be clear."

"Worse," he replied. He immediately got on his headset. "We are under attack. Make sure you sound the alarm. Meditrina needs to know what is going on, then grab your weapons and go meet them. Now."

SIXTEEN

S age and Thomas continued their fight to the death while Meditrina and her minions watched with eager anticipation. Money was subtly beginning to change hands as the stakes grew. Thomas and Sage were sweating and tired. They were both doing everything they could not to make a fatal mistake.

But they both knew the truth. They were moving slower, and it was only a matter of time before one of them made a mistake. Then it would end quickly.

"Do you think they care who wins?" Sage asked Thomas as she swung her sword, just missing his chest.

"Odd time to strike up a conversation," Thomas replied, breathing heavily. He lunged forward with his axes and went for Sage. He was still upset with her. It could have been so much easier. She blocked his attack and quickly went back on the offensive.

"Sage, they want to see your blood, and they know I am capable of doing it." He blocked her attack, following it up with a countermove. Sage cringed as the ax nicked her side. The vampires cheered at the sight of blood.

"Even if there is the slightest chance you win, they will never let you out of this place alive," Thomas said.

Sage charged after him, sword swinging.

"Now it looks like a real fight," Meditrina said, downing her cup of red wine. The crowd cheered Sage's charge.

"They just want to see blood," Sage said to Thomas. "They don't care if it's yours or mine."

"Will you two just shut up," said Meditrina, looking for something to throw at them. "Stop talking, and start killing." This provoked a roar of approval from the crowd and a newfound energy from Thomas. He charged Sage, and she let the momentum he had take over. She dropped back and tossed him into the front row of the crowd.

Thomas got up and looked at Sage. He shoved a few chairs out of the way as well as a vampire who hadn't been clever enough to move when he should have.

"They want a show." Sage shrugged, brushing some hair away from her face. "I guess the crowd just got the best of me." The crowd pushed Thomas back into the fighting area.

The two warriors stared at each other. They were tired, beaten up, and bleeding. Although Meditrina was enjoying herself, the fight was beginning to bore her. "Enough of this. One of you just kill the other already," she said. "Wait. I have a better idea. Why don't we have Sage's friends join this little fight? Edward, bring the rest of them upstairs. Now."

ROWAN SAT IN her cell wondering what was going on. She hated being stuck here like a caged animal. Her transformation had only held so long. Now she was back to normal, although the energy she had used had taken a lot out of her. She began to pace. Pain shot up her leg, reminding her that her ankle was still tender.

Liberty was lying on the ground, almost asleep, but began to stir when Rowan started moving around. "Rowan, are you okay in there?" she shouted.

"Just getting antsy," Rowan answered, still covered in sweat from transforming back to a human. "I have this thing with being locked up. I just don't like it."

"The animal in you is really starting to shine through," Liberty said. "Maybe we can use it to get us out of here?"

"I don't know, especially since I tried it already and most of my energy is gone," Rowan said nervously. "This hasn't happened in a long time, and I don't know how I'm going to react in the next minute or so." Rowan had a fear of being contained, and it was even worse when it was a cage. This all came from an incident that happened during her younger days of being a werewolf.

Liberty sat on the floor of her cell, pulled her legs up to her chest, and began to rock. "Simon, do you happen to have any ideas on this one, buddy?" Liberty asked. There were two loud knocks on the wall. "I'll take that as a 'no.' That's what I thought."

Rowan was still pacing, her skin beginning to prickle and itch. "Liberty, we need to find a way to get me out of here real soon, or we might have a situation on our hands."

"Hey, guard," Liberty shouted through the bars.

"You need to wait a minute," he said. "I'm taking a call."

"You better get here now and deal with this situation. I'm talking pronto," Liberty said. "Guard," she called again.

Finally the guard made his way toward the cells. "What do you want?" he shouted, keeping his distance.

"We need to get her out of here," Liberty said, gesturing to the cell where Rowan was pacing. "She's starting to freak out, and I don't know what she's going to do."

"What do you care? She's in a different room. The only one that she can harm is herself." The phone rang again, and the guard went to answer it. He spoke softly into it for a few minutes, then walked back over. "It seems like you are going to get your wish after all." Rowan and Liberty looked at the man in silence.

"What do you mean?" Liberty asked.

"It appears the events that are going on upstairs aren't festive enough. They want the three of you to join the party."

HAZEL HAD BEEN sitting in the truck watching things in the club through the camera system. Before Gabriel made any move with the attack on the club, they had decided that it would be best for him to carry a communicator.

"Gabriel," Hazel called to him as he continued with the battle going on outside.

The battle was heated and unlike anything Hazel had ever seen. Vampires and angels battled to the death. Hazel began to wonder if this was even close to what would happen when the final battle between good and evil took place. Gabriel finally answered, "Go ahead, Hazel. What did you catch on the monitors?"

"We have a new situation developing. It seems they are moving Rowan, Liberty, and Simon to the main hall with Sage. Any ideas on how to handle this one?"

"I'll have to take some of my team and go after them. Things will become a whole lot more difficult if they make it to the main hall."

Hazel paused and then said, "Makes sense to me."

"If we wait until they're in the main hall, we'll have wide open spaces where we're more likely to get attacked, not to mention more people to deal with."

"Then I will find you the easiest way to get down there."

"Good," Gabriel said as he slashed the chest of a vampire who had gotten too close to him. "Let's make it quick. We don't have a lot of time."

"LET'S GO," THE guard shouted at Liberty as he brought her out of the cell. As her eyes adjusted to the sudden light, she saw that she was in a hallway with the guard that had been keeping an eye on them, as well as several others, to make sure they stayed in line.

"You mean it's time for the big party, and you aren't even going to give me a chance to dress up," Liberty remarked. It was a defense mechanism: sarcasm was the easiest way for her to hide the fact that she was actually scared.

"No, but someone sent a special request to take you up there," the guard said. He knew what was going on up there, but he had no intention of telling them the truth.

Liberty's questions were answered all too soon when Francis walked in the door.

"Hello Liberty," he said with a snarl, happy to have a chance to go after her again. "I brought you something special for the occasion." He held up his hand; a pair of handcuffs swinging from one finger.

"That's so sweet. Exactly the style I was hoping for."

He tossed the cuffs to her, making her put them on. Afterward, he walked up to her and made sure they were on nice and tight. He leaned forward and whispered in her ear, "Still planning on killing me sometime tonight?"

"The night is young," she whispered back. "I still have plenty of time."

"We'll see about that." He pushed her down into one of the chairs. "Let's get your other friends." They pulled Simon out of the cell and found him half dressed. "Well, lover boy, it seems like the ladies did a number on you after all." Simon didn't respond. His eyes were focused on Liberty, who was looking at him, mouth ajar. Francis glanced at Liberty. "I guess you didn't know." He laughed. "He got caught in the lady dancer's dressing room. They had their way with him and then turned him in." Liberty quickly turned away. "It seems like the two of you may have been more than just traveling companions. Well, not anymore."

"Did you really have to do that?" Rowan shouted from her cell. "I think you enjoyed that a little too much."

Francis glanced into the cell and laughed. "Coming from someone who is in your situation, I would watch how you talk to me." He looked to the other guards. "Take the harness and the tazers and get in there. If she gives you a hard time, shock the hell out of her. Got it?"

The vampires nodded but remained where they were.

"I said go," Francis shouted, and they all scurried inside. Rowan screamed, and there was the sound of a scuffle. After a moment, Rowan walked out of the room with three nooses around her neck, followed by one of the guards with his tazer.

Francis watched as Rowan was taken out. "It seems as if Meditrina wants you to enjoy some of the festivities. Especially the fight that is going on between Thomas and Sage. It is my job to take you up there. There will be no talking, signing, or any other forms of communication. If I see anything out of order you will have to answer to me. Do you understand?"

No one answered.

"I said, do you understand?" He had other things that he would rather be doing but he got stuck on this detail.

"Yes, we understand," Liberty said, since Simon couldn't speak and Rowan was too shaken up by the tazers to answer.

"Good."

THERE WERE FIGHTS breaking out all over the building. The main club room had angels battling vampires, and the two were quickly eliminating one another. It was a medieval battle of supernatural proportions and it was a sight to be seen.

Back in the main room, an exhausted Sage and Thomas who were equal matches for each other were given a surprise by Meditrina.

"Stop," she shouted, standing up. The two fighters stopped and looked at her, arms still raised to strike. "It is obvious that you two are not going to kill each other anytime soon. So here is my new plan: I am hav-

ing my security bring the intruders to watch what is going on." She started to pace the area and watched the crowd, making sure that they hung
on every word she said. "Here's where it gets better." She smiled. "When
they get up here, I will give you the command to begin fighting once
more. The only difference is, if either one of you doesn't kill the other at
the ten minute mark, I will kill one of your precious friends. I will kill
one of them every ten minutes until they are all dead. If neither one of
you is dead in that half hour, I will personally kill you both. This is going
to put new meaning in the phrase 'sudden death.' You see? I have a sense
of humor also. Catch your breath while you still have the chance, because
things are about to get interesting."

FRANCIS LED THE group down the hallway of the prison
area and back up the stairs to the main hall. Rowan knew that Sage was
in a battle to the death with Thomas, and that they were going up there
to sweeten the pot. The only wild card that was left in this whole thing
was Hazel. Their fate was left in the hands of a new techie that didn't have
any experience fighting, let alone planning rescue missions.

Just then they heard a loud crash, causing everyone to jump. They
could hear the fighting and knew something was up. Rowan felt hope
bubble up in her chest.

"Maybe Hazel came through," Liberty whispered to Rowan.

"We can only hope. She's all we've got right now," Rowan said a little too loudly.

"Keep it quiet back there," Francis said, stopping the line of prisoners abruptly. He walked over to Rowan and Liberty and stared both of
them down. Rowan was just starting to regain her senses, so she returned
his stare without fear. With a flick of his head toward the vampires holding Rowan's noose, the rope tightened around her neck. Rowan yelped
and dropped to her knees, pain in her eyes.

"Stop it! You're going to kill her," Liberty shouted.

Francis looked at Liberty and then addressed the vampires. "Bring her over here. They aren't going to care if one of them goes missing." Two of the guards brought Liberty over, making her kneel in front of Francis. Simon and Rowan immediately began struggling against their bonds, with no luck. "Since you walked into this building, you have been nothing but a pain. I should have killed you the first time I laid eyes on you. I won't let this chance escape me again." He pulled out the hunting knife that Liberty had been using before she was captured. "Recognize this? I found it lying on the floor. Your time is about to end," he said, pulling the knife back to strike.

A scythe materialized, creeping around Francis's neck. A voice echoed straight through Francis, causing him to stop dead in his tracks.

"You go through with it, and I turn your head into a basketball."

Liberty looked up and saw someone that she didn't know standing behind Francis. Liberty smiled as the blade completely circled his neck.

"You don't know who you are messing with," Francis said.

"No, it is you who doesn't realize who they are messing with," Gabriel replied. "I am Gabriel, and these are some friends of mine." He looked to Liberty with a smile. "Hazel called for us, and we answered. So what's it going to be? Do you really want me to show your friends here how sharp this blade really is?"

"Since your offer is so convincing…" Francis said to the surrounding people, knowing this was his last stand.

Liberty sat there, down on her knees, watching everything unfold. Things weren't looking great at the moment. She put herself in Francis's shoes and knew there really wasn't much he could do to get out of this alive. So if he was going down, he might as well take someone with him. At least that's what she thought he might do. All she knew was that she wasn't ready to die. She closed her eyes and waited for her fate.

Francis drove the knife downward, putting all his anger into one violent arc. Just before the knife reached Liberty, Simon threw himself in its path. At the same time, Gabriel followed through with his scythe. In one clean sweep, Francis's head left its body and landed right next to Simon and Liberty with a bounce. Liberty opened her eyes, not knowing what she was going to see. All she knew was that she'd heard blades go through flesh twice. Francis's detached head faced her with its eyes closed.

Liberty brought her hand up to her chest and felt liquid. She looked down at the blood covering her hand and began to panic until she realized that it wasn't her blood.

"Simon," she shouted. Simon had taken the shot right across the carotid artery. He was bleeding out quickly. Gabriel tried to find something he could do to help, commanding the others to kill the remaining vampires and free Rowan.

"Simon... Why did you have to go and do that? That was so stupid, you're so s-stupid." Tears rolled down Liberty's face, mixing with Simon's blood. She lowered him to the ground until she was cradling his head in her lap.

The angels freed Rowan, and she knelt beside Liberty, screaming for someone to help. "Someone start ripping cloth. We need to slow down the bleeding." Rowan was already ripping Francis's shirt, handing the strips to Liberty. "Apply pressure to the wound. We have to stop the bleeding."

"There's a pressure bandage in my bag. Maybe that will help," Liberty said, looking around for her bag. Each strip of cloth that Liberty pressed to Simon's wound was blood-soaked and useless in less than a minute.

The angels rounded up the others in the security detail. Once the vampires realized what had happened to Francis, they gave up pretty quickly. With the rest of the vampires essentially incapacitated, some of the other angels stopped what they were doing to watch Rowan and Liberty work together.

"It's like nothing I've ever seen before," said one of the angels. "Sworn enemies, working together to save a life."

Rowan grabbed the pressure bandage out of Liberty's bag and quickly unraveled it. She was about to hand it to Liberty when she noticed how soaked in blood the girl was. "Kid, you are a mess. This isn't looking good," she said.

"I don't care," Liberty said. "We have to save him." She never took her eyes off Simon. "Why did you have to do that?" she murmured.

Rowan gently raised Simon's head so she could put something under it. She knew, now, that he wasn't going to make it. She wanted to make sure he at least had some comfort.

Simon, who was having trouble doing anything, raised his hands and began to painstakingly sign to Liberty.

I'm sorry, he signed.

"For what?" she said, applying the dressing to his neck, slowing the blood just a little bit. "We can talk about that later, after we get you out of here."

Simon shook his head. He raised his hand, and for a moment Liberty thought he was trying to sign something else. Instead, he lay it over her heart and looked deep into her eyes.

"What you did for me, Simon. I—" Her voice broke as fresh tears appeared. "You jerk," she said, gently punching him in the shoulder. "You picked the worst possible moment to do something heroic and sweet like that. You could have just given me flowers, or something. It would have been a lot easier."

Simon laughed silently ,and then grimaced at the pain.

"What is it, my friend?" Gabriel asked, kneeling beside Simon.

Simon motioned Gabriel closer. He signed something that only Gabriel could see.

"I understand." Gabriel got up and motioned for Rowan to follow him. When the two had moved a short distance away, Gabriel spoke. "Rowan, we need to move on if we want to save Sage."

"I know, but what are we going to do with the two of them?" Rowan asked.

"Simon said to get her out of here. He doesn't want to see her cry."

"But what if she doesn't want to go? I wouldn't leave if it were me." She would want to stay until his last breath.

"He's not giving her a choice. This is his last wish. He doesn't want her to see him die in pain."

"Why?" For that moment, Rowan was the closest thing to human in a long time. "No one should die alone. He can forget the whole tough guy act."

"I know," Gabriel said. By the way he looked at Rowan she knew that no matter how hard she fought that there wasn't going to be a way to change this. "But this is his wish, and I'm going to make sure that it is followed."

"Fine, what's the plan?"

"I'll tell her. Then we leave. Grab her, if you have to, and we'll go," Gabriel said.

"You are the one that's going to have to deal with her then," Rowan said as they made their way back to Liberty. As they approached, Rowan noticed that Liberty had draped herself over Simon's body, her own body wracked with her sobs. They heard a heart-wrenching moan as they approached.

"He's gone," Liberty said. "He said good-bye, closed his eyes, and then he was gone."

"I'm sorry, Liberty. Simon was a good man. I'm proud to have fought on the same side as him," Rowan said.

"I realize this sounds cruel," Gabriel said, "but if you want your shot at some revenge, come with us and we will get back at the ones that are responsible for Simon's death."

Liberty looked up, Simon's blood smeared across her cheeks, mingling with the tears running down her face. "If that's what I have to do to honor Simon's memory, I'll do it."

Rowan looked over to Gabriel, breathing a sigh of relief. "That was easier than we'd anticipated."

"As long as when we get out of here we take Simon with us," Liberty said, clinging tighter to Simon's motionless body. "There is no way that I want to leave him here after tonight. This place will be a burial ground for evil, and he's better than that."

"Agreed," Rowan said.

"Understood, you two have gone through a lot together," Gabriel added. "Let's get going. The other team will be in position within the next ten minutes, so we need to move." He stopped for a moment. "And before we go any further." Gabriel handed communicators to both Rowan and Liberty.

Rowan pressed a button and began to speak. "Hazel, are you there?"

Hazel cheered, then laughed. "It's good to have you back with us."

"It's good to be back." Rowan was still shaken up from the harness around her neck and the tazer, but she was quickly recovering. "You've done some great work here, Hazel."

"Thanks. While you were gone I made some new friends," Hazel said jokingly.

Rowan chuckled. "I see that, and it's a good bunch as well."

"Liberty?"

"Yes, Hazel?"

"I am so sorry about Simon. I know you cared about him."

"Thank you," Liberty said. "He liked you, you know. He thought you were interesting."

Rowan got back on the communicator. "Hazel, without you things would have been a lot worse. So, thanks."

"Yes, thanks. You're pretty cool. For a human," Liberty said.

"Thanks, everyone," Hazel said.

"You know, if you ever change your mind and want to become a vampi—"

"Not this time, Liberty. I'm happy with who I am. Now, get this job done. Kill Meditrina and get Sage back."

Gabriel motioned the women closer. Time was running out, and no one was sure how much time they had before Meditrina grew bored of waiting and killed Sage herself. "All right," said Gabriel, "here's the plan."

SEVENTEEN

The starlit sky shined through the atrium that covered most of the room in the main hall. At the far end of the room Meditrina sat with her feet up, trying to figure out if there was a way to salvage a victory out of tonight. On the other side of the room sat Sage, and not too far away from her was Thomas. Meditrina was bored with the fight, so she decided to give them time to catch their breath.

"If no one kills the other in the next ten minutes, I will be obliged to kill you both. My friends want to see blood, and I would be a bad host if I didn't acquiesce."

Sage stared at Thomas, wondering if this was what he'd thought he was getting into when he'd set his plan in motion.

He looked up at her. "What?"

Sage shook her head. She felt sorry for him. He had wanted power, and look where it got him. He could end up losing it all, and at this point, Sage was going to need to make sure that he was dead if she wanted to make it past the morning.

"Is this how you expected things to go?" she asked him. As much as she despised Thomas, this wasn't the way for someone to go.

"I'm sorry," he said. Quite suddenly he looked very human and very old. He was defeated, and Sage knew it. If she finished him off, at least he would die with dignity. If Meditrina did the job, neither of them would be granted that. "I didn't want this at all. Now I'm going to have to kill you if I want to get out of this alive." He looked down at his two short axes. "Don't worry," he said, the vampire returning in full force, "I will make it quick and finish you off so it won't be painful."

Sage smiled, showing the confidence that had gotten her this far in life. She turned her chair to face him. "When I kill you, Thomas, it's not going to be quick at all. And I am going to make sure it hurts as much as possible. You tried to play the game with the wrong woman, and now it's time for you to burn."

Thomas looked frightened for a moment, then he grinned. "You see, you're more like us than you think. You like the blood and violence just as much as we do. You should have taken her offer. You should have become one of us. You should have let me turn you. Heck, I should have just turned you regardless. You would have come around." Thomas stood up.

"I would have come around after I killed you. But there's something that you'll never understand." Sage stood also. "The one thing that makes you and me different is that when you mess with my friends, you mess with me. When you hurt my friends, you hurt me." Sage was tired of playing games. She was ready to get this over with, to finish what they'd started. "I say let's give these vampires what they came here for. If they want blood, then let's give it to them." She pulled out her sword and charged.

Meditrina smiled. Thomas instinctively met Sage's charge with his axes. He lifted his boot and kicked Sage in the stomach. All the air rushed out of her, and she crumpled to the ground. She gasped for breath, a sharp pain radiating through her chest

Thomas looked down at her, watching her struggle to suck air into her lungs. A snarl formed on his lips, and Sage finally got to see the vampire side of him in full force. "You want to stop playing? That's fine with me." He kicked her in the ribs, flipping her onto her back. Sage cried out in pain. "You want tough? I will give you tough." Thomas kicked her in the side again, but this time she grabbed hold of his foot, and tossed him over her. Thomas hit the ground, and without missing a beat, he drove his heel backward into her chest.

"Wow," Meditrina yelled from across the room. She pointed to Sage and to Thomas as the crowd cheered at the action. "It seems that Thomas decided to man up and finally fight the woman that has been besting him."

Thomas sneered at Meditrina and took a moment to catch his breath. He raised his axes and charged Sage, who was only just beginning to get up. She caught sight of Thomas out of the corner of her eye and rolled to the side, causing his own momentum to carry him forward until he tripped over one of the chairs, landing in a heap. Without missing a beat, he stood up. Anger contorted his face, and he threw one of his axes at Sage. He knew that the move could cost him if he missed, but he didn't care. The ax found its mark in her thigh. Sage screamed as the pain shot through her body as though someone had just set her leg on fire. She tried to keep calm, to see past the pain, but she dropped to the ground. She began to panic and tried to pull the ax out of her thigh. Thomas smiled as the smell of her blood reached him. The crowd smelled the blood, too, and began to chatter, eager with anticipation.

"It seems our combatants have decided to make this fight more interesting," Meditrina said as she sat back in her chair. "Now all I need to see is Francis with those prisoners. Maybe we won't have to use them after all." She looked to the crowd and laughed. "Who am I kidding? I say we kill them anyway." The crowd cheered at the idea of more blood being spilled.

Sage struggled with the ax as Thomas moved closer. She shimmied backward, doing her best to put more distance between herself and Thomas.

"What's the matter, sweetheart?" Thomas said as he wiped away the sweat from his eyes. "You've never run away like this before. You thought I was your friend." He laughed and took aim with the second ax.

"You know she will just kill you the minute you step out of line, right?" Sage said, trying to get him to think about the bigger picture.

"If that's the case, then I am still going to go down as the one that killed Sage McKenzie. I will still be a legend."

Just then the door opened with a slow creak. For a few moments, silence followed. Meditrina called out; she was tired of waiting. "Francis, it's about time you got here. Were the prisoners giving you trouble?"

Someone threw something into the room. It bounced twice and rolled into the center, leaving a bloody trail. Some of the vampires began to scream when they saw what it was. The head came to a complete stop in the middle of the carpet. Sage used their distraction to her advantage and got back to her feet.

Meditrina slowly got out of her chair, staring at the head on the floor. When she realized it had belonged to Francis, she bent over and picked it up. She held it level with her own face. "Apparently he was in over his head trying to handle them." She laughed manically, maintaining eye contact with the severed head the entire time.

"Someone bring me another chair," she commanded. When one of her stooges obeyed, she circled the chair as she spoke. "Francis, since you screwed up and lost your head over this whole situation, you should see how this all turns out." She slammed the head down in the seat next to her. "Does anyone have a problem with that?" she demanded, looking out into the crowd, waiting for an answer. "That's what I thought."

Meditrina spoke quietly, directing her words to Francis's head. "People need to see what happens when they don't follow a simple order and get the job done. Incompetent, that's what they are."

She grabbed her glass of wine and drank, and then spoke loudly to the room. "This means the prisoners are loose. Why isn't anyone going to find them and bring their heads back to me? Hello, I need some of you to start moving and acting like vampires!"

THE DOORS SWUNG open, revealing Gabriel, Rowan, and Liberty, flanked by several angels.

Meditrina glanced over to Francis's head. "These are the ones that got the better of you. You call yourself the head of security?" She looked to the group that had just entered the hall. "What are you doing here?"

Rowan stepped forward and glared at Meditrina. "You invited us. All we are doing is taking you up on the invitation. We also happened to run into some of our friends along the way, so we figured you wouldn't mind having some extra guests."

"Well," said Meditrina, once again speaking to the dismembered head, "I hope you're happy, Francis. This is all because you couldn't complete this simple task." She suddenly screamed, knocking over the chair with the head on it. "Why is it that I am having such a hard time getting some good help around here? All I wanted to do tonight was to kill a bunch of humans, take over the town, and see those two..." She pointed to Sage and to Thomas. "...Kill one another. Is that too much to ask for?"

"I'll make this easy for you, Meditrina," Gabriel said, stepping forward. "You and your vampires need to surrender and hand Sage back over to us. You do that, and we won't have any issues."

Meditrina took a step back. "Gabriel, it's nice to see that I was important enough for them to send you and your team to help out. But if we don't surrender?"

"You will all die." Gabriel smiled and reached for his weapon.

Meditrina laughed. There was no fear in her eyes. She already knew what it was like to live in Hell and there was no way she was going to go back. "Do you really think I'm scared of you and your group of rebels?" She stood up and gestured to all the other vampires in the room. "If you haven't figured it out by now, let me point something out to you. You are outnumbered." She spoke slowly, as though she were talking to children. "Just kill them. Kill them all," she ordered.

All hell broke loose in the main hall. Gabriel, Liberty, Rowan, and the angels pulled out their weapons, ready to take on the oncoming horde. Some of them had weapons while others came baring their teeth.

Even with the angels on their side, they were still outnumbered. Rowan's heart began to race. She loved everything about this moment: she loved the smell of battle and the fact that she had the chance to shed some vampire blood. There were several vampires she wanted to kill personally. Still, things didn't look good.

"We need to draw as many of them as we can out to the center of the floor with us," Gabriel said to the others in the group. He held his scythe aloft and took off two vampire heads in one clean sweep. They flew across the room, hitting the oncoming vampire horde like a bowling ball hitting pins.

"Why?" Rowan asked, taking out one of the vampires with a shot from her sais straight to his heart.

Hazel jumped in on the communicator and said, "Everything has been planned out just for this situation. Just be ready when Gabriel tells you, because it's going to get messy real quick."

Liberty, who was going one-on-one with some vampire, joined in. "You mean you guys were expecting something like this?"

"Yes," Hazel said, pride lacing her words. "And we already have something in mind that will even up the odds in just a bit. Do as Gabriel says, and it will be fine."

"You heard them. Bring as many as you can into the middle of the floor," Rowan said to everyone.

Liberty noticed Gabriel keeping a close eye on the window. "What are you doing?" she asked.

"Don't worry. It's almost time," he said, fending off a sword that was swinging at him. He turned on his heel, barely escaping a vampire's fangs in his neck.

Rowan was under attack by two vampires. She managed to shake off one, but the other managed to tear into the flesh of her arm. "Argh!"

she yelled, and then looked over to Gabriel. "Whatever you've got going, do it now."

The vampires kept coming. It seemed as if they were multiplying. Bloodlust ran through them, making them even more dangerous.

Meditrina simply sat on the chair in the front of the room, watching the action and cheering her minions on. "That's it," she yelled, her glass of wine still in her hand. "Come on, get him." The vampires were dropping in numbers as well as the angels. "You guys should be killing them a lot quicker. I want their heads, especially Gabriel. Whoever gets his head will get a big reward." Her offer excited the frenzied vampires even more, sending them into overdrive.

SAGE LEANED AGAINST the pillar for a moment, knowing that if she was ever going to attack Thomas again, this was her moment. "Here goes nothing," she said. Nephilim were able to heal fast, but it wasn't instantaneous, and the pain from the ax was still giving her trouble. Thomas had his back to Sage, trying to decide if he should join the vampires or not. He turned around just in time to see Sage barreling toward him. She threw her shoulder into his stomach and drove him down onto the floor. Once she had him there, Sage drove a knee into his groin for good measure.

"You're not the only one that can play dirty," she said with a smile as she watched Thomas cringe in pain. She stood, looking down at him. She was still favoring one leg, but she was ready to fight.

She reached down, took her angel's wings, and opened them up from her belt. "You've always wanted to get close to me. Now you have your chance. Get up," she yelled at him. Thomas cautiously pulled himself to his feet. He looked for his axes and found them close by. He picked them up, and the two of them squared off once more, knowing that this was going to be the last time they would both be standing.

"To the end," Thomas said as he took a deep breath. There was a part of him that really didn't want to kill Sage, but the way the cards played out he knew that he had no choice at this point. It was kill or be killed, and Thomas wasn't ready to die.

GABRIEL GLANCED AT Liberty. "It's time. When I give you the signal, I want you to get out of the room."

"Why?" Liberty asked, finding a second to speak between oncoming attacks. "I want to keep fighting."

"Some of my friends are dropping in. For your protection, you need to be out of here." Gabriel motioned to the large glass window above them. "Trust me, you don't want to be here."

Hazel spoke up. "I know what's going on, and if I were you I would listen to him." Liberty nodded in agreement.

"Now, Liberty. Run!" he shouted. She followed his orders as four vampires followed her out of the room.

Gabriel glanced at the skylight and hit the button on the communicator. "Hazel, it's time we let a little light into this place."

"I'm with you. I'll tell the others," she said, thrilled to be the one to call the final charge.

"If I were you I would get under my wings," Gabriel said to Rowan. She did as he suggested. A loud crashed filled the room as the skylight exploded. Rowan looked up in time to see a dozen angels coming in through the top of the building. They soared with their wings spread wide. The glass rained down, and Rowan realized it was no longer night. The light was coming in through the hole in the window.

"That's why you wanted Liberty out of here," Rowan said to Gabriel. He nodded in agreement.

"She's on our side, so I had to protect her," Gabriel said as they continued to watch the glass fall. Rowan was still protected by Gabriel's wings.

"Are you okay?" Rowan asked Gabriel.

"I'm fine," he said. "Some glass just landed wrong on my wings."

Rowan noticed spots of blood among the pure white feathers. "I know that's not all vampire blood. You need to pull them in," Rowan demanded. "I'll be fine."

"No," he said, "it's just about over, and then we are back on the attack." They watched the rest of the glass fall.

There was something very soothing about watching the angels land. Not to mention that the direct sunlight streaming through the hole in the window made a great equalizer. Vampires screamed as the sunlight caught those that couldn't get away. Rowan watched as the sunlight burned their flesh, turning them into piles of ash.

Rowan had never seen anything like this. "So this is how it's going to look when the final battle happens."

Gabriel looked at the scene, watching the angels take out vampire after vampire. He saw the chaos of battle, along with the bloodshed of both his friends and his enemies. "It will be similar in a lot of ways. But in other ways it will be much worse than this. Things are starting to settle down. We need to move, or we'll be sitting ducks."

"I'm ready whenever you are," Rowan said. "We still need to find Sage."

"That's the easy part." Gabriel pointed across the room to where Thomas and Sage were locked in battle

"Then let's get going," Rowan replied.

LIBERTY RAN FOR the hall as soon as she heard the glass breaking. She was surprised to see vampires following her out of the room. She sprinted down the hallway, focused on getting to Simon's body. She turned the corner and slid to a stop, almost tripping over a dead body. It wasn't Simon's, however, and a cursory glance over the rest of the dead vampires confirmed his absence.

"No, no, no. Where is he?" she said. She didn't have time to search for him. The four vampires that had followed her were catching up. She looked around for a place to hide. The footsteps grew louder, and Liberty was on the brink of panic when inspiration struck. She laid on the floor and pulled a dead body over her.

It wasn't too long before the vampires arrived. They only stayed a moment before three of them sprinted down an adjacent hall. The fourth one remained as though waiting for her to come back that way.

Liberty waited until he turned away before pouncing. "Where is he?" Liberty sat on the vampire's chest, hand at his throat.

"What are you talking about?" the vampire asked, his bloodshot eyes wide.

"Don't play games with me," she said as she slashed his face with her nails. "Where is the body of the vampire that was killed here?"

"I have no idea what you're talking about." Liberty could tell he was a young vampire, unaccustomed to battle.

Liberty couldn't accept his answer. She slashed out at him again. This time, she got his neck and managed to put a nick into the carotid artery. "There was a vampire that was killed here, and we left his body right over there. Now it's gone. I'll ask you again, where is he?"

"I don't know," he said, pleading. "I don't know a thing about that. I've been inside the main hall the whole time."

"I don't care," she said to him. Anger, rage, and complete sorrow filled what little soul she still had. It was the closest to feeling human that Liberty had felt in a long time. It felt freeing. She loved being a vampire, but she had forgotten what it felt like to have your heart break. She had lost complete control, and the loss was somehow freeing. "I just want something other than what I feel right now." She bent down and latched on to the vampire's neck and ripped away at the flesh that covered his throat. This was it. This was how she could let go of what she was feeling.

The blood felt like fine wine running through her body and made her forget about the world around her. She took in as much blood as she could; it felt like a blanket as it spread through her body. She felt good—

at least for the moment—as she licked the blood off her fangs. Then it all started to creep back in. The pain, the anger, and the rage. She needed to get control back, or she needed to find something that could help her not feel. Blood would be the easier of the two to find right now. She could worry about getting the control back later.

She debated between hunting down the three vampires who'd run off or waiting for them in her previous hiding place. Someone knew where Simon's body was, and she was determined to find out. She just needed to be sure she didn't make her plans obvious.

SAGE FELT SOME of her strength returning at the sight of angel after angel pouring in through the broken skylight.

"The cavalry has finally arrived," she said and lunged toward Thomas.

Thomas was tired and struggling. One of his axes ended up stuck in a nearby pillar. "This is far from over," he said, watching Rowan and Gabriel make their way over. "It looks like your friends are coming to help." Thomas turned toward Rowan. "I thought you said you always gave the ones you hunt a fair chance. You consider three-on-one fair?" Thomas called out to a few vampires close by and motioned for them to join him.

"We gave you a fair chance. If we hadn't, you'd be dead already." Rowan stared at Thomas. "Believe me, I could easily do it." She turned to Sage. "I thought you said I was going to be able to kill him."

"Rowan, this isn't the time for that," Gabriel said. "We need to let them finish this. Alone." He pointed to the other side of the room where Meditrina sat, lazily watching the fight. She saw Gabriel and Rowan looking in her direction, and she waved.

Rowan said, "She's a little more than crazy."

"That sounds about right. I need to go check on Liberty. You keep an eye on Sage." Gabriel pointed to two oncoming vampires.

Without hesitating, Rowan pulled out her sais and charged the oncoming vampires. The distraction gave Sage the advantage, and she managed to drive her angel wings into Thomas's sides.

"Damn you," he said. His remaining ax clattered to the floor as he grabbed his sides. "It wasn't supposed to go like this. All you had to do was take the offer." He fell to his knees.

Gabriel stopped and watched Thomas fall. He noticed Sage's sword glinting on the ground a few feet away. He scooped it up and tossed it to her.

"It would be easier to finish him off with this," he said.

"Thanks." She looked at the sword for a moment before her gaze drifted back to Thomas. Blood was oozing through Thomas's fingers, and he knew he was done. "I know you said you wanted to make this slow and painful, but I am begging you. Can you please just stop and finish the job?"

Sage knew that she needed to do it. Knew that it would have taken a cruelty she didn't possess to let him die like that. Still, she was hesitant. He had his flaws, like anyone, but it was more than that. He'd chosen to continue down the path of evil. Sage held her sword, ready to strike.

"This is what happens when you try to serve two masters." In one swift motion, Sage swung Dragon's Claw and took off Thomas's head. It flew back into the fighting crowd, and his body fell forward to the ground. "You end up losing your head over it," she said and then fell to the ground, exhausted.

Rowan made quick work of the two vampires she was fighting and ran to Sage's side. "Are you okay?" she asked. She took in the wounds on Sage's shoulder and leg. "On second thought, you look bad."

Sage looked at her and smiled. "Good to see you too, pal."

Hazel got on the communicator. "It's good to have you back with us, Sage. You had me worried."

"It's good to be back, guys. I was a bit worried myself. Hazel, you pulled a small miracle. How did you think of that?"

"I don't know," Hazel said. "I just asked for help, and then Gabriel showed up. He is very cool."

Gabriel, who still had his communicator on, heard and responded, laughter in his voice. "You're pretty cool yourself, Hazel."

"I forgot you were on here, too. I can't believe that you heard that."

"It's probably not the first time he's heard it," said Sage.

"Don't worry about it, Hazel. She is right; I have heard it a lot. Still haven't gotten used to it," Gabriel said. "But now, I need to check on Liberty." He switched the communicator off.

EIGHTEEN

Liberty lay underneath the pile of dead vampire bodies. The smell reminded her of rotten meat. She lay there waiting, covered in their blood. She didn't care. It was her chance to find some answers. Someone had to know where Simon was, and she didn't care if she had to kill the whole lot. She was going to find out and then get him back.

Then, it was the taste of vampire blood. It was helping her. It was the first time that she had tasted the blood of another vampire. It made her forget everything for a little while. She needed this. Better yet, she hungered for it. To get it and take the vampires out, along with some answers, was a win.

A sound came from the hall where the three other vampires had disappeared. She was about to be able to kill again, and that was a relief to her. The whole time she sat there, waiting for something to happen, her emotions had took control once more. They hit her like a brick to the side of the head.

Now she was ready to taste that blood again. She began to wonder if this was what it was going to come down to. Was this what she had to do so she could go on without Simon? She was going to have to become a vampire killer. It didn't sound good to her, but neither did the pain and emotion that she was feeling. The footsteps were getting closer; she heard them loud and clear. She heard the heartbeat of the vampire that was approaching. The chance to forget was almost here. She timed her strike with the steps, and then when she felt he was within reach, she jumped without warning, taking him down to the floor.

This time the vampire was stronger and began to fight back. He managed to kick Liberty off him and get back to his feet. Liberty didn't see a vampire in front of her. She saw an opportunity to release her pain and anger. That was enough. She sized up her opponent and knew that she was going to have a hard time taking this one on. He was bigger than the first, and she'd lost the element of surprise. It didn't matter. If she couldn't take him, he would kill her and that was also fine.

She had to make a move. It was now or never. Her heart began to race, and she had just decided to charge when there was the sound of a blade cutting through the air. The vampire dropped to his knees as his head fell forward and almost rolled over Liberty's feet. She stopped and saw Gabriel standing behind the vampire, scythe in hand.

Gabriel looked at Liberty as if he were ready to strike again if he needed to. He slowly lowered his weapon and raised his hand toward her.

"By the name of Jesus, demons that are in her body, I bind you and tell you to leave. You are not welcome inside her."

Liberty stirred and felt something tugging at her. She looked at him. "What's going on?" She was suddenly very frightened.

"It's okay," Gabriel told her. "I'm freeing you. There is a demon that is trying to take hold of you, and I'm not letting it. Liberty, you need to understand that it's okay to grieve."

His words struck her right in the heart. She needed to grieve.

"It's not fair," she said. "He died trying to save me, and only then do I realize how I truly felt for him. It's too late now. And they've taken him away from me. I came back here like you said, to check on where I hid him, and he's gone." The blood-red tears began to run down her face, and she fell to her knees, sobbing. "They took him, and I want him back."

"He's gone?" Gabriel asked. "Let's go and look at the spot where you hid him." Liberty led him to where she had hidden Simon. It was a good hiding spot and almost impossible for someone to find. They really had to have been looking to find the body. Gabriel searched the area, trying to find something that would give the slightest clue to what happened to him. Just as he stood up to move away, he noticed something on the wall.

"It can't be," he said and went to get a closer look. Liberty followed. "Look at what this says."

Liberty looked at the markings on the wall and read out loud:

I will find you—S.

A smile spread across her face. "He's alive. He must have had enough strength to get out of here so he could bury himself. Now he can heal."

"That is incredible."

"I need to find him and help him if I can," Liberty said, already walking away.

"No," Gabriel shouted after her, but she was too far to hear. Gabriel watched her disappear. There was no way to stop her. What she was feeling was far too powerful. He was just worried that her chances of finding Simon were slim.

MEDITRINA WAS GETTING desperate. Her whole plan was crashing around her. Everything had been going right until Gabriel had come in with the angel reinforcements. She would have to find another time to deal with him. Glass covered the ground where half the angels entered through the skylight. Angels were on the offensive, aggressively taking on the vampires. The vampire numbers were dwindling quickly as well as Meditrina's dreams of domination, and with the death of Thomas, there was nothing left keeping her here.

She wondered if she could go somewhere else and start over. Somewhere far away from this place and the incompetent help. She managed to find two vampires to help her get away from Sage, who was hot on her trail. "I don't care what you do," she told them. "Just make sure you give me enough time to get out of here." They acknowledged her and charged at Sage with their swords raised.

Sage didn't waste a moment. She met them with her sword, taking the brunt of the attack. Meditrina was vulnerable. She was going to do what she could to make sure she could capitalize on the moment. Sage countered their attacks with a kick to one of the vampire's stomachs and then took out the second vampire with the claw of her sword to his heart. He fell to the ground with a thud.

"One down, one to go," she said, turning to face the other vampire. He looked at her and knew he was in trouble. Still, Meditrina had given him orders.

Sage caught sight of something out of the corner of her eye. Meditrina was sneaking out of one of the secret exits. Sage activated her headset. "Hazel are you there?" Sage swung her sword up to meet her opponent's sword with a deafening crash.

"It's nice to hear you back on the communicator," Hazel said. "What's going on? And are you okay?"

"I just saw Meditrina on the run, and yes I am okay. I need to know where she's going, and how I can beat her there." Sage battled the remaining vampire, taking a shot from his oncoming sword. "Hurry up, Hazel. I can't let her get away. Especially after everything she's done."

"Boss, it doesn't look good. Whatever you do, you are not going to be able to get there in time."

"Damn it," Sage shouted, taking the head off the vampire she was fighting in one swift motion. "I can't let her get away like that. She told me she knows how to find my father. I need to get that information from her." Sage was getting desperate and began pushing through the crowd to get to the door that Meditrina had disappeared through.

"Sage, it will never work," Hazel said. "I don't care how good you are. She is going to get away."

"Then what should I do?"

"Let me slow her down," she said, suddenly.

"No," Sage replied immediately. "I will not allow that. You have no idea how to deal with her. Heck, you have no real idea how to fight at all."

"What other option do we have? I will slow her down until you can make it out there and finish her off."

Sage tried to find the latch to activate the secret door. Rowan made her way over to Sage. "What's going on?" Rowan asked. "Did she just say that she wanted to go after Meditrina herself?"

"Yes, she did."

"That's crazy. Hazel, stop being crazy," Rowan said over the communicator.

"I know," Sage said. The door swung open.

"But she's right, Sage."

"Don't tell me you are going to side with her on this. How do you exactly suggest she stop Meditrina?"

"Look, she doesn't have to stop her. All she needs to do is slow her down enough for us to catch up," Rowan said. "Make a decision about this before it's too late."

"Damn it, Hazel, what are you doing? I hear the truck running. Are you on your way to find her? Sage asked.

"Sorry, Sage. You can take this up with me when we finally take care of Meditrina," Hazel replied. She parked the truck and switched off the communicator.

Rowan and Sage looked at each other, the chill of panic running down their spines. "We need to move now," Rowan said.

HAZEL KNEW THIS was a bad idea. She also knew there was a chance she would get hurt doing it. She parked, took a deep breath, and stepped out of the truck.

She looked around until she found a large trash bin. This was where Meditrina's secret path would lead. Hazel ran to the spot she'd chosen to hide and crouched down to wait. She felt like her chest was going to explode. The combination of fear and adrenaline was a bit overwhelming. She kept her eyes on the spot where Meditrina was going to come out while practicing her slow breathing to relax. It was something she had seen Rowan do when she was getting ready to practice, so she figured it would work for her, too.

Hazel noticed the secret door beginning to open. It opened very slowly; it must have been years since the door had been opened. Hazel crept down behind some garbage cans and waited. Finally, Meditrina stepped out. She exited the passageway slowly, cautious about the sun, but it was overcast now. Meditrina must have rated the risk low, because she stepped out and began walking.

Hazel began to throw pebbles at the back of Meditrina's head, praying that she wouldn't kill her on principle.

"What the hell was that?" she said as she turned with her hand on her head. "Whoever you are, you just need to stop it. Hazel, is that you? You finally came out of your fortress of solitude?"

Hazel screamed when she charged Meditrina. She hadn't planned on screaming. She hadn't really been planning to charge, but seeing this woman in the flesh, this woman who had killed so many, and yet wandered free, made Hazel's blood boil. Before Meditrina could react, Hazel was on her back, holding on for dear life.

"What in the Devil's name is going on here?" Meditrina tossed Hazel off her back like a sack of potatoes.

"Meditrina." Hazel got up, catching her breath. "This is my one opportunity to get my hands on you."

"Child, you need to walk away while you are still alive." Meditrina looked down at Hazel in disbelief.

"Sorry, there's no chance of that happening." Hazel got to her feet.

"I should crush you right now," Meditrina said. "However, since you've shown me that you've got some fight in you, coupled with the fact that you are too young to know better, I am going to be the one that walks away. Now be a good girl and let me do that." Meditrina turned and began to walk away.

"No," Hazel said. "Don't walk away from me like that." Meditrina stopped and turned to look at Hazel.

"Fine. You've got me. Now what are you going to do?" Meditrina asked.

Hazel froze, drawing a blank on what to say or do.

"That's what I thought. You are nothing but a little coward." Meditrina turned on her heel to walk away.

Hazel ran after Meditrina and once again jumped on her back. She used a choke hold that Rowan had taught her. Meditrina fought back, and Hazel hadn't realized how strong she would be. Finally, when Hazel realized that the hold wasn't working, she took her hands and placed them on the side of Meditrina's ears and yelled, "I wish that every time you close your eyes you would see the pain of all your victims as well as hear their screams." All of a sudden Meditrina felt a pulse run through her body. She let out a scream that sent a chill down Hazel's spine. Meditrina tossed Hazel off her back and into a nearby wall. Hazel's head hit the wall hard, and she fell to the ground, unconscious.

Meditrina cracked her neck as she approached Hazel. "You stupid little girl, you wanted to play with the big dogs and look what it got you. Your plan failed as well." She walked closer to Hazel. "Watch." Meditrina closed her eyes to demonstrate, and then she quickly opened them back up. "What the—" She did it again. This time she began to see the pain and hear the echoes. "No, this can't be!" The screams got louder. "She couldn't have done this." She looked down at Hazel, who still hadn't moved. Meditrina kicked her, trying to wake her up. "Damn you! You need to wake up and fix this," she screamed at Hazel's motionless body.

Sage and Rowan, hearing the screams, burst through the door. They saw Hazel lying on the ground.

"No," Rowan yelled and charged straight at Meditrina. She transformed into a werewolf before she even reached her. Sage followed behind, opening up her angel wings.

Meditrina turned around just as Rowan launched herself at her. The two of them hit the ground hard, and Rowan strained her mouth toward Meditrina's throat. Her claws scraped at Meditrina's skin but left little damage at first. Meditrina's vampire skin held up well against the werewolf claws. Meditrina attempted to throw Rowan off her with everything she had. She looked straight at Rowan and stared into her wolf eyes.

"Are you crying?" she asked, catching Rowan off guard, which was all the distraction Meditrina needed to toss her off. She stood and looked down at Rowan. "You were crying. You actually care for these people. I commend you for that, but it will only get you killed in the end." She turned away, hearing the faint sound of a scream echoing in her head.

Sage stood ready to throw her wings at Meditrina, but stopped when she noticed she appeared to be having some sort of fit. She was clutching her head and telling "them" to stop screaming. On an impulse, Sage reached out to her.

"Are you okay?"

Meditrina looked around. She couldn't tell what was in her head and what was really happening. "I can't fight like this. I will get her back for doing this to me." She pointed to Hazel on the ground and then covered her ears, trying to shut out the screams echoing inside her head. She closed her eyes and saw the faces that belonged to the screamers. "You should save your friend. Everyone...everyone that I attacked...that I killed."

Rowan and Sage looked at Hazel, who still hadn't moved. Rowan began to transform back into herself.

"You haven't heard the last from me," Meditrina said, and put her hands to her ears. "Just make the screaming stop." Then she ran as quickly as she could and disappeared in the distance, hands still covering her ears.

Rowan finished transforming and ran to Hazel's side. "Come on, kid," she said, wiping the tears from her eyes. "What did you have to do that for?"

"She wanted to prove something to you," a familiar voice said from behind them. Sage and Rowan turned around. It was Gabriel. He looked tired, and his scythe was covered in blood. "She wanted to make sure you knew she was the right person for the team." He looked down at Hazel. "She was trying so hard to find a place just to fit in."

"Of course she is," Sage said, coming back to reality and kneeling next to Rowan.

Rowan turned and looked at Gabriel. "Can you do something?"

"This request is coming from you of all people?" he asked.

"Desperate times call for desperate measures."

"This is no time to worry about whether we converted her or not," said Sage. "Can you help her?"

Gabriel moved closer. "Let me see what I can do." He laid a hand over her and began to pray. His prayer was unlike any prayer said by humans. He prayed as someone who had lived and seen the things that the Creator could do, someone who had seen the power and the glory. He began to pray and did it with genuine love. Sage and Rowan felt it radiating off him like energy. It was so strong that the two of them had to take a step back. Once he was done praying, he leaned in and whispered something into Hazel's ear, kissing her on the forehead. He stood up.

"Get her someplace safe. She should be coming around in no time."

"Thank you," Sage said, standing beside him.

Rowan followed and offered her hand to Gabriel. "Thank you. I don't know how...just thank you."

"You are both welcome," he said with a smile. "Let me go out there and see if I can delay the authorities from showing up until you are ready to leave." He nodded to them and then his wings unfolded, and he flew up and out of sight.

Rowan said, "That was pretty cool. I'm glad we're on their side."

"Me too," Sage said.

"What the heck," Hazel said, holding her head and groaning as she sat up. "I feel like I was hit by a truck."

"More like a whole fleet of trucks that ran into a brick wall," Rowan said. She knew that she needed to be careful about telling her too much. She didn't want to overwhelm her anymore today. "Welcome to the land of the living."

"What happened?" Hazel asked.

"Gabriel brought you back after Meditrina threw you into a brick wall and tried to kill you. But I will say what you did to Meditrina in return was pretty incredible," Sage said, still amazed by what she had seen.

"Was I dead?" Hazel asked, her voice breaking.

"I don't know," Rowan said to her. "You were quickly heading in that direction. Good thing we have some friends in high places."

"Amen to that," Hazel said. Then she realized something. "So that's who whispered to me."

"What did he say?" Sage asked.

"It begins today."

NINETEEN

Sage walked through the empty meeting hall, checking for anything good that she could collect and send back to her accountant. She saw a necklace with several jewels and reached down to grab it.

"I wouldn't do that if I were you," a voice spoke from behind her. Sage, still in battle mode, turned quickly with her sword drawn. She stood face-to-face with Gabriel. "They are evil, but it is still stealing."

"I need to keep this operation running somehow." Sage bent down and grabbed the necklace off the fallen vampire's neck.

Gabriel laughed as he watched her. "You're always going to go to the beat of your own drum," he said, turning a blind eye to what he'd witnessed. "Just make sure the offering is extra good this time."

Sage was caught off guard. "Um….okay. I'll make sure of it."

Gabriel looked shocked. "You mean you haven't, Sage?"

"Well…you see…" Sage said, tripping over her words as she tried to explain herself.

"Just make sure you take care of it this time." Gabriel sounded almost like a parent. "What kind of example would that be? Besides, it looks like you may have made some headway on both of your teammates."

"At least one of us thinks that," Sage said with some uncertainty.

"Don't worry, it will happen in their own time," Gabriel told her.

The two of them started to head outside to catch up with the others. Sage said, "I wanted to thank you for coming to our rescue."

Gabriel turned toward her. "Remember, that was all Hazel. She is the one that called for me. I only answered. You need to make sure that you thank her."

"I know."

"Take care of her and teach her well. She has a lot of potential, and you don't want her to waste it."

"I agree, and I think Rowan will make sure that I don't."

"Rowan has taking a liking to her," Gabriel said.

"Yes." Sage smirked. "I think Rowan has finally found that little sister she's always wanted."

"That's good to hear," Gabriel said.

They finally made it outside and both surveyed the work being done to clean up the Asylum. There were people loading up dump trucks and those taking care of any injuries. Sage knew there was still a major concern about Meditrina. Nobody knew where she'd gone, or if they were ever going to see her again.

Gabriel said, "You know, this is only the beginning."

"Of what?"

"The war that is coming. Sage, we need you on our side. We need you committed to fighting evil the way we fight evil. You need to remember that when we fight we see no shades of gray. You're either with us or against us."

"This is the part where you tell me that you need me and my team on your side so we can end evil once and for all?" Sage asked.

"Yes, but you are still not the toughest being out there. You need to be ready, and depend more on your team and less on yourself. Do that and you will be fine. You will make it to the endgame."

"Thanks," Sage said, and the two shook hands, which became an embrace. "I still need to do things my way right now, but I will keep it in mind, I did really enjoy having the cavalry come and save the day."

"You really haven't seen anything yet," Gabriel told her. "That was only a sliver of the stuff we can do."

Hazel made her way toward Gabriel. She was still shaken up from her scuffle with Meditrina, but she was slowly heading back to her old self.

"Feeling better?" Gabriel asked, studying her face.

"I think I am starting to feel more like me again," Hazel said. "But I got a nasty bump on my head, and I still have a lot of questions about what went down."

Gabriel looked to Sage.

"What you did to Meditrina was basically like a psychic transference," Sage told her. "You sent all the terrible images and energy that you could muster to her head."

"And what you did," Rowan said joining the conversation, "was just plain crazy." Hazel looked down and gave a half shrug. Rowan smiled and said, "It was also one of the gutsiest things I have seen a human do in a long time."

Hazel's face lit up. "Thanks."

"Do it again without the proper training, and I'll hurt you myself," Rowan said.

"I didn't even know that I was able to do it."

Gabriel looked at her. "I don't think Meditrina knew you were capable of something like that either. I also don't think she is going to forget about it for a long time. I would make sure to start your training and better the skills that you already have."

"There are a lot of things that you never realized you were capable of," Sage told her. "Finding out what they are is all part of the training."

Gabriel walked over to Liberty who was sitting alone, gazing across the road ahead. "I am sorry about Simon."

"Thanks," Liberty said with a smile. "He was good."

"I know," Gabriel told her. "That will help him."

"I still can't figure it out. What happened to him? How could a body vanish like that?"

"It isn't the first time something like that happened."

"Do you think there's a chance?" Liberty asked. A glimmer of hope shined in her eyes.

"I have seen stranger things happen," Gabriel said. "What are you going to do now?"

Liberty stood up and grinned. "I'm going to see where this road takes me. Besides, if he is out there and still alive then we will find each other again."

Gabriel nodded. "Just be careful what you do when you come to that fork in the road."

"I will. Besides, it will give me a chance to see some places that I've always wanted to go. Hey, Rowan." She motioned her over. "Come on, you crazy chick. Are you going to say good-bye or what?"

"Leaving so soon?"

"Did you really think I would take a spot on Sage's team?"

Rowan said, "You have a point. Man, I am really starting to get soft." She looked over to Hazel. "Do you see what you're bringing out in me? I actually like this one." Rowan pointed to Liberty.

Hazel grinned and waved. "I like her too, and you're welcome."

Liberty looked at Rowan, suddenly struck by an idea. "Why don't you come with me? Thomas did say when the werewolves and vampires come together there's a lot of trouble."

"It is a tempting offer, and I do think we could have some fun, but I can't. My place is here with Sage and Hazel. This team is really good, too." Rowan smiled at Hazel.

"Suit yourself. I don't think any of our kinds would understand us anyway. We are both pretty crazy chicks," Liberty said. The two of them laughed and hugged. They let go and quickly looked around to make sure no one had seen them.

Hazel caught Liberty right before she left, remembering something that she wanted to ask her. "The sunlight, isn't that going to—"

Liberty shook her head and chuckled. "Hollywood messed that up. Well, at least most of them did. It's the direct sunlight that can put a big hurting on us. Luckily for me, today has cloud cover. I should be fine until the afternoon."

Hazel gave Liberty a hug. "Stay safe. Good luck and good-bye."

"I don't think this is the last time I'll see you guys. So all I'm going to say is…catch you later, kids. I'm out of here." Then with the blink of an eye, she was gone.

HAZEL MADE HER way toward Gabriel. "Are we going to see you again?"

"Don't worry," he said. "I am going to be around for a long time."

Hazel smiled. "That's good to hear. I still have a lot of questions."

Gabriel looked down at her. "Hazel, you have some really good teachers. You need to listen to them. They will make sure you grow and do well."

"I know," she said as she looked out and saw Rowan and Sage waiting for her. "They've had some influence on me already."

Gabriel smiled. He leaned down and kissed her on the cheek and whispered in her ear. "You will find who you are supposed to be. You were meant to be great. And remember," Gabriel said as he took Hazel's hands and held them together, "when you need help, all you have to do is pray." He glanced over to Sage, who had heard the exchange. Hazel looked up at Gabriel questioningly, and he winked at her.

"Thank you," she said as she blushed. No one had ever talked to her the way he did. It was new, and Hazel wasn't used to it. Gabriel walked off as Hazel watched. His wings spread, and although it was overcast, they were still beautiful and glistening in the morning light. He turned one more time to his friends and waved. They all waved back. He began to run. Once he'd gained some speed, his wings began to move, and he took off.

Hazel, her eyes on Gabriel, said, "If I stick with you guys, I'm going to get to see cool stuff like this all the time?"

Sage and Rowan thought about it for a few moments.

"Yeah," Rowan said.

"Pretty much all the time. You'll see even cooler stuff," Sage said.

"Cooler than that? I'm so in."

"Then we're ready to go," Rowan said, wanting to start up the truck.

Suddenly, Sage had a bad feeling in her gut. She felt like she was being drawn back inside.

"Are you okay, Sage?" Hazel asked.

Sage got off her bike. "I'll be right back. I need to go and check this out." She walked toward the Asylum, uncertainty lacing every step.

"I don't like this," Rowan said.

"I don't either," Hazel chimed in.

"Believe me, I don't like this much myself." Sage drew her weapon. "If I'm not back in ten minutes come and get me."

SAGE WALKED BACK into the Asylum, moving quickly. It wasn't going to be long before the police and the fire department arrived on the scene. She knew that a lot of the remnants from the battle would have disappeared into the wind by the time they got there, but the smell was really bad, a metallic tang that Sage could never truly get used to. She covered her mouth as best as possible while still wielding her sword.

"Whoever the hell you are, you got me back in here. Now you need to show yourself and then we can get down to business." Sage waited, but heard nothing. The smell was really starting to bother her, so she turned to leave. In the darkness, she bumped into something. She quickly turned, and thinking that it must be one of the vampires that hadn't been killed, she swung her sword blindly at the obstruction. He saw it coming and caught the sword in his gloved hand, smiling. Then he tossed the weapon aside.

"I wouldn't do that if I were you," the man said. Sage finally managed to get a good look at him. The man standing before her was tall and broad. His face could have been chiseled from stone, and his look was just as cold. He was not a vampire. Vampires didn't have any real beauty to them; they were essentially monsters. The man standing before her wasn't a monster.

"What are you going to do about it?" Sage said. She dove to the ground, picked up her sword, and rolled out of the way as the man's foot narrowly missed her stomach. She jumped up and swung her sword at the man's chest. Just before it made contact, he vanished and appeared right behind her.

"I'll just make you look foolish," he said as he reappeared. Sage swung at the man again, only to find she was swinging into empty air.

"Stop that, you are only making me more angry," Sage said. He had reappeared behind her, and she attacked him once more. He disappeared again.

"Doesn't the saying go three strikes…" He gestured, and Sage's sword went flying out of her hand. "…And you're out?"

Sage pulled her angel's wings out and once again the man disappeared before she could get a single blow in.

"Stop it," he yelled at her.

"Why?" Sage continued to search for an opening, a weak spot. Finally, the man put up his hands, and Sage froze. She couldn't move, and felt as stiff as a plank of wood.

"Because I am only here to talk to you. Sage, I like your work. I don't really care that you managed to take out some good followers of mine. I also like the fact that you managed to unite that werewolf and a vampire."

"How do you know who I am?"

The man looked a bit relieved. "Now we are finally making some headway." He noticed that Sage was still trying to get herself loose from his grip. "Will you be good if I release you? If I let you go, and if you are good, I will tell you everything. Can you do that?"

Sage nodded begrudgingly. "Fine."

He looked pleased and released his hold on her. She immediately grabbed hold of his fine clothes and said, "Now talk."

"Still feisty, even when the odds are against you. That's what I've always liked about you, Sage. Still, nothing like your father. Definitely one of your mother's traits."

"Who are you? What do you know about my parents? Have you been watching me?"

"Your father is one of mine."

Sage felt the darkness flow from him and got the chills. "It looks like my stock has gone up. A visit by the Devil himself."

"Call me what you want—I am the Dark Lord, The Prince of Darkness, Satan, Shaitan, whatever name you know me by, it is all the same in the end because here I am in the flesh." The Devil bowed as he spoke.

"What do you want with me, Devil?"

"Please, if you need to call me a name just call me Lucifer. First off, 'he' wants you to join their side in this upcoming war, so of course I want you. I have come to make you a deal."

"A deal…" Sage glanced around for an exit. "Did you see what happened to the last person that tried to offer me a deal?"

Lucifer spoke with a similar eloquence that Meditrina had. The voice was silky and mesmerizing, diffusing before going in for the kill. "It comes down to this…I need you. Several of my followers are starting to get too powerful."

"Why don't you just eliminate them yourself?"

Lucifer looked at her in shock. "And cause chaos in my ranks? Do you think I should show God and his angels that there is a chink in the armor? Come on, Sage, 'he' is still completely under the impression that I am in complete control down here. I need to continue to show 'him,' as well as the rest of the human world, that I am in control. Meanwhile, the world has gotten so much darker, what used to be considered evil has become much more acceptable. Look at what they watch on TV and see in the media or on the street corner. I do have control down here."

"How are they becoming threats to you?"

"A threat to me as well as to our whole kind. There is a whole different world out there. People are smarter and are looking to find out more," Lucifer said. He paced as he talked, and acted like he was continuing to educate her in how the world works.

"Why don't you just show them you exist and then we can move on?" Sage asked.

"Don't you remember how the Salem witch trials went? The worst part of that was how many of them weren't witches. Do you want that much persecution but on a grander scale? It would be like the Crusades all over again. I am enjoying the control that I have, and I don't plan on giving that up any time soon." He laughed. His confidence was high, as if he thought he had exactly what Sage wanted.

Sage looked at him, interested in what he had to say. She found it fascinating since someone from both sides of the fence had come to see if she would play with them. "What is this deal that you mentioned?"

The Devil began to weave a web of deceit. "We help each other. You do my dirty work, and I will lead you to your father."

Sage was taken off guard. This was the second time she'd heard this offer in as many days. "Why would you want to help me with my father?"

The Devil began to pace. "I never liked him. I never liked what he did to you and your mother. It just wasn't the right way of going about it. Besides, he is on my list."

Sage began to wonder how long she'd been in here. Surely Rowan would come looking for her soon. As though he'd read her mind, Lucifer said, "Don't worry about your friends. I took care of the time situation. Time is going much slower for them. We'll have plenty of time to talk."

Sage decided to sit down and get comfortable—this was the Devil himself. He of all people should be able to back up what he was saying. What reason did he have to lie to her? She knew all of his games and what he was about. And she was interested in hearing what he had to say.

"Why should we eliminate them?" Sage asked, caught up in the power that the Devil had.

"If I don't eliminate them, when the time comes for the final battle between good and evil, I will have too many minions with a different agenda then mine. The result will not be satisfactory."

"So police your own and exist quietly in the shadows," Sage said, realizing what the Devil was thinking.

"Exactly."

"Why should I trust you? I trusted Thomas and look where that got me. If it wasn't for the invasion of *Vampire Beach* I would have been dead."

The Devil laughed. "Or worse…a vampire."

Sage realized how ironic that would have been and laughed.

"You can't trust me, Sage. You know who I am. I can still tell your instincts are buying into this idea, and that is a good thing. I have nothing to hide." He stood up and opened his suit jacket, revealing empty pockets.

"You may be right but to make a deal with the Devil never ends well."

The Devil was smart. He was a master of manipulation, and Sage had never really dealt with someone like him. And he knew what she was about, what she stood for, and what buttons to push to get her to do what he wanted. He was prepared for this discussion and had something up his sleeve that he knew Sage couldn't resist. He reached into his previously empty pocket and pulled out an envelope.

"How about this? Here's some information about one of the names that are on my list." He handed Sage the envelope. It was bigger than a regular one, but still small enough to fit inside his pocket. "You will find the situation very familiar, something close to home. If you find her in time you will find someone just like your father to take down. Consider this a chance to correct a wrong that was done to you. Besides, he is one of those angels that managed to escape with your father. Then you will see that I have no underlying scheme in this whole thing. I see a business opportunity, and I am looking to make the most out of it. We will talk again sometime after that."

Sage tore into the envelope. She scanned the sheets inside and got a jolt like a knife to the heart. "You bastard, hit me with something like this right off the bat."

The Devil laughed smugly. "I am the Devil. We'll be in touch?"

"We will." They shook hands, and Sage felt sick to her stomach.

The Devil looked at her and smiled. "You know, we could make one hell of a team." He laughed once again and then vanished.

Sage looked down at the pictures and saw a mother and daughter, and knew what she had to do. Her pulse quickened. "You can say that again." She put the pictures back into the envelope. "Well at least we know where we are going now."

HAZEL AND ROWAN couldn't wait any longer and made their way inside.

"Do you think we gave her enough time?" Rowan asked as she made her way past Hazel, pulled out her sais, and headed down a hallway.

Hazel ran to catch up with Rowan, doing her best not to stumble. "I was just thinking the same thing."

"Look, you should probably wait by the truck. You did take a nasty bump on the head."

Hazel shook her head. "I'm fine. I want to make sure she's okay. What happens if there is more trouble?"

"I'll take care of it," Rowan said.

"Yeah, that's true. I will let you lead then," Hazel said, dropping back behind Rowan. The two girls heard some rattling from a nearby door. "What was that?" Hazel asked nervously.

"I don't know, but I think we need to check it out," Rowan said. "For all we know that could be Sage."

They crept up to the door and looked at each other. Hazel spoke up, "You're going to open it, right?"

Rowan looked at her. "I'm the one with the weapons, what if something jumps out? Are you going to get it?"

Hazel looked at her like she was crazy. "No."

"Sometimes it amazes me that you got as far as you did in life."

"That was just wrong," Hazel said. "I'll get the door." She reached over, unlocked the latch, and managed to open the door and jump behind Rowan all in one motion. The door slowly opened with a loud creak. The women took a few steps inside.

"Wait," Rowan said to Hazel. "I've got an idea." She reached into a pocket and pulled out a glow stick, which she opened and cracked. "Now at least we can see what's going on." They took the glow stick and aimed it into the room, which was actually small enough to be a closet. In the back of the room, a set of eyes stared back at them.

"Is someone back there?" Hazel called out. She shined the light toward the back and revealed a girl in her mid to late twenties, sitting in one of the corners with her knees pulled in toward her chest. She looked like she had been in there for several days. Her hair and clothes were a mess, and she had been crying. Right next to her was another girl about the same age.

"Are you okay?" Rowan asked.

"No more," the first girl said. "You took all the blood out of her that you could without killing her. You promised. You said you would leave her alone."

Hazel's heart went out to the girl. "We're not here to hurt you. We're friends."

"Hazel, be careful. This could be a trap."

Hazel glanced back at Rowan and rolled her eyes.

"This is just crazy," Rowan said as she watched Hazel head deeper into the room. The girls sat in the corner, scared and unsure, not knowing who to trust. "Let's get them out of here." Rowan headed into the room to get closer to the girls. The one on the floor was still asleep, but the other girl had backed herself into the corner.

"It's okay," said Hazel. "The whole thing is over."

The girl looked to her with a gleam of hope in her eyes. "It's over?" she asked, ready to collapse at any moment. Hazel looked at the girl and for a moment she saw her sister again.

Rowan smacked Hazel on the shoulder to bring her back to reality. "Yes, it's all over. No one is going to hurt you anymore." The girl began to cry as Hazel helped her and walked her out of the room. Rowan went and got the other girl. Once outside the room, the girl looked at Hazel with wide, haunted eyes, and asked, "Can we go home?"

SAGE REALIZED THAT he was gone. She let what had just happened sink in. "This is nuts," she said. "Maybe they were telling the truth when they said a war is coming." Sage got her sword and made her way out of the room. Sage knew this could change a lot. She wanted to make the best decision for Hazel and Rowan, but the temptation to take the Devil up on his offer to help her find her father was strong. Sage made her way out of the building. She needed to get out of there. She didn't know how much time had passed since her conversation with the Devil, and she didn't know if the others would be looking for her.

ROWAN AND HAZEL were sitting with the two girls, trying to figure out what to do with them.

"Do you girls have names?" Hazel asked, doing her best to emulate Gabriel's calm, caring voice.

One of the girls looked at Hazel and then back to Rowan. She was deciding if she could trust them. She hesitated, and then finally spoke up. "My name is Tara. And the other girl is Lisa. We went to this club about…I don't even know how long ago it was. All I can remember is that we met some guys, and we were having a good time with them. They bought us some drinks, and the next thing we know we woke up here." Tara began to cry again.

"It's okay. You don't have to worry about that. It doesn't matter how long you've been here," Hazel said.

Rowan and Hazel looked at each other and shook their heads. They may have met some vampires that they liked, but the vampires who had tortured these women were pure evil. Rowan hoped they would die a slow and painful death. She heard a noise, and she kicked into fighting mode. She grabbed her sais and looked at Hazel.

"You stay here and keep an eye on the girls," Rowan said. "I'll go and check that out." Without hesitation, Rowan was off.

"Don't worry, she'll be right back," Hazel told Tara. "One of our friends is still in here, and we had to come back in to get her." Tara nodded, and Lisa began to wake up. "How are you doing?" Hazel asked.

Lisa was still weak and groggy. "Okay." She realized she wasn't alone and began to panic. Hazel and Tara managed to calm her down and caught her up on what had happened in the last few moments.

"You mean this whole nightmare is over?" Lisa said, and then broke down.

"Yes, it is." Hazel gave her a hug.

ROWAN WAS HEADING toward where she thought she heard the noise with her weapons drawn. "Sage," she said at a whisper. "Is that you?"

Sage came out from behind a set of shelving, putting her weapon away. She was still stuck on what had just happened. "You will not believe who I just had get together with."

Rowan looked at her with interest as she put her sais away. "Since you've become Miss Popular, I have no idea."

Sage looked at her. "It seems the Devil is interested in having us come and work for him." She handed Rowan the envelope.

"What's this?" Rowan asked as she opened it and looked at the pictures.

"It's what the Devil gave me to show that we can trust him," Sage told her as they began to walk back.

"I don't get it."

"The pictures are of a mom and young daughter. The Devil gave me the location of another one of the fallen angels that escaped with my father. He wants us to go after him, says he has gotten out of control and it's a situation I know too well," Sage said.

"It's you all over again? This time he is giving you a chance to make the save."

"He is giving me the chance to be the one thing I didn't have in my situation," Sage said. "How long was I gone?

"It was about ten minutes. We were just heading in to find you. Why?"

"I was in that little chat for at least twenty minutes. He said he did something that slowed down time for the two of you," Sage said.

"Wow," Rowan said. "A nice trick, but I don't know if we should be playing with fire like that. All I know is, whatever faith you believe in, if you make a deal with the Devil you only end up getting burned."

"I know what you're saying," Sage said. "But once again he offered me a chance to get to my father."

"They get you on that every time," Rowan said to her. "When are you going to realize that? You need to understand that getting him is going to come at a cost no matter what you do. What you need to decide is what cost are you willing to pay?"

"That's why I'm glad you are around, Rowan," Sage said. "Someone needs to make sure I stay in check. Still, this one was a freebie, and if there is any truth to this one, we may have to check it out."

"We will have to discuss that later. I have something that I need you to check out now."

"What's that?"

"Hazel and I found something. Or, someone, I should say."

"Really, who?"

"Just come with me," Rowan said. "It proves what I thought about this club. What I was saying to Thomas has a bit more credibility then we thought."

"All right, let's go."

ROWAN BROUGHT SAGE to where Hazel and the two other humans were. Sage shook her head in disbelief. "If they were in there, who knows how many others we might find."

That was something that Rowan and Hazel hadn't thought of. Hazel knew Sage was probably right. "I guess we'll have to check all the rooms, won't we?"

"We'll have to be really quick," Rowan said. "It's only a matter of time before we have some company on the scene.

"I'm going to get the girls out of here. You guys finish checking around."

Sage looked at Hazel. "Are you going to do what I think you are?"

"Yes," Hazel said. "I can make them forget about the whole thing."

"Just make sure that you're careful," Sage said. "We don't need—"

"What happened to my sister won't happen again," Hazel said, forcefully ending that part of the conversation.

"There's no need for that, Hazel. All I was going to say was that we didn't need anything to happen to you."

"Oh." Hazel blushed. "Sorry."

"Let's make this happen," Sage said.

"What was that about?" Rowan asked Sage as they made their way back into the building.

"One of her psychic gifts is that she is like a sponge. She can absorb the emotions of someone, and she has done that in the past to help her sister when they were younger. The only problem was that she overdid it and wiped out too many memories."

"That's horrible."

"What made it worse was her sister even forgot who she was," Sage told her. "The only thing that she could do was leave her at an orphanage, and then she made a deal with some group called the Truth. It's supposed to be some super-secret group that deals with making ordinary people extraordinary through science."

"So Hazel is not a true psychic?" Rowan asked with some curiosity.

"She is," Sage continued. "She's just more powerful then she wants to be. She doesn't know how to handle the powers and really didn't want them in the first place. But it was the only way she could make sure that her sister was protected and safe."

"Does she know where her sister is?"

"The only one that knows is the head of that group. Some guy named Xander McPeek," Sage told her.

"Wow," Rowan said, showing a bit of sympathy. "That's pretty harsh, but it still explains some things about her."

"She managed to get away from them," Sage told her, "and figured the only way to find her was to become a hacker. But as far as her gifts, she has been afraid to try it since then. This is the first attempt that she really has had to use it since then."

"Let's hope she has learned how to control it better," Rowan said.

"I know she's gotten better."

Rowan looked at her as she closed the door. "The only way we are going to get more rooms checked out is if I change." Rowan stepped away and began to transform into a werewolf.

"Just be careful," Sage went on. "If things get out of hand, I want you to get the girls and get out of here. I will take care of whatever trouble happens. We don't need to freak them out any more than they already are."

ROWAN AND SAGE made their way outside to the truck after a few minutes with one young man who had been in the wrong place at the wrong time. Hazel looked at the small group of humans. "At least they were equal opportunity takers," she said. "Bring him to the back of the truck. I'll take care of him and then we can put him with the others." They began to hear police cars in the distance.

"How are the other girls?" Sage asked Hazel.

"They're sleeping," she said. "When they wake up, they will have no recollection of the horror that they went through." She looked over to the young man that was still visibly shaken from what he'd gone through. "Do you want to forget this whole thing?"

He nodded.

"Good," Hazel said. "Let's go for a walk." She took him by the hand and led him away.

"Where does she put all the emotion and garbage that she absorbs?" Rowan asked Sage.

"I don't know. That's where I have to work on helping her before something bad happens."

"Like what?" Rowan asked as she got in the truck.

"No idea," Sage added and then yelled to Hazel as she got on her bike. "Come on, we need to go now."

Hazel slammed the back door of the truck and made her way to the other front seat. "He's out like the rest of them. Where to now?"

"We leave them somewhere safe, let someone know where they are, and then get out of here," Sage said as she started up her motorcycle.

"About the letter…" Rowan trailed off, waiting for Sage to explain.

"We will talk about it on the way."

"Will someone get me caught up?" Hazel asked.

Rowan looked at her. "I will explain it."

Hazel looked over to Rowan and said, "Hey, I thought of another one that could be a good nickname—"

"Just give that a rest," Rowan said with a smile.

Hazel laughed. "I was just messing with you."

SAGE'S ✝ CROSS

CONTINUES

THE HERO PROJECT
A SAGE'S CROSS PREQUEL

REDEMPTION
BOOK TWO

 ABOUT THE AUTHOR

E.M. is a storyteller at heart, and believes that there is a bit of truth to all myths and legends. He has a broadcasting degree, spent thirteen years in the Army reserves, and is a Thyroid Cancer Survivor. He left the east coast for a slower paced life in the Midwest.

www.ingramcontent.com/pod-product-compliance
Lightning Source LLC
Chambersburg PA
CBHW020623180626
46810CB00007B/2914